DINOSAUR

KYLE MEWBURN & DONOVAN BIXLEY

MEGASAURUS MASH-UP 1

BOOKS 1-4

SCHOLASTIC

AUCKLAND SYDNEY NEW YORK LONDON TORONTO
MEXICO CITY NEW DELHI HONG KONG BUENOS AIRES

T-WRECK-ASAURUS

STEGO-SNOTTYSAURUS

PAGE 101

VELOCITCHY-RAPTOR

DIPLO-DIZZYDOCUS

Arg's Valley

1. Pterosaur Cliffs
2. Lava Mountain
3. Bog
4. Slimepot Swamp
5. Big Bone Lake
6. Village Fire Pit
7. Arg's Village
8. Stinkooze Pit

A Grogllgrox
a tribe of
bloodthirsty caveman

Old
Drik

Gurg

Shlok
Arg's best friend

Arg
Caveboy genius

Krrk–Krrk
Arg's pet
Microceratops

Arg's
Grandad

Arg's mother   Arg's father

Hng
Arg's big sister

The author would like to point out he doesn't really believe Neanderthals and dinosaurs lived at the same time. He certainly didn't see any dinosaurs when he visited the Stone Age in his time machine while researching this book.

This four-volume edition first published in 2013 by Scholastic New Zealand Limited
Private Bag 94407, Botany, Auckland 2163, New Zealand

Scholastic Australia Pty Limited
PO Box 579, Gosford, NSW 2250, Australia

Text © Kyle Mewburn, 2011
Illustrations © Donovan Bixley, 2011

ISBN 978-1-77543-170-1

National Library of New Zealand Cataloguing-in-Publication Data

Mewburn, Kyle.
Megasaurus mash-up. Book 1 / by Kyle Mewburn ; illustrated by Donovan Bixley.
(Dinosaur rescue ; 1-4)
ISBN 978-1-77543-170-1
[1. Neanderthals—Fiction. 2. Dinosaurs—Fiction. 3. Humorous stories.]
I. Bixley, Donovan. II. Title. III. Series: Mewburn, Kyle. Dinosaur rescue.
NZ823.2—dc 23

12 11 10 9 8 7 6 5 4 3 2 1   3 4 5 6 7 8 9 / 1

Publishing team: Diana Murray, Penny Scown and Frith Hughes
Design and layup by Donovan Bixley
Typeset in Berkeley Oldstyle
Printed in China by RR Donnelley

Scholastic New Zealand's policy, in association with RR Donnelley, is to use papers that are renewable and made efficiently from wood grown in sustainable forests, so as to minimise its environmental footprint.

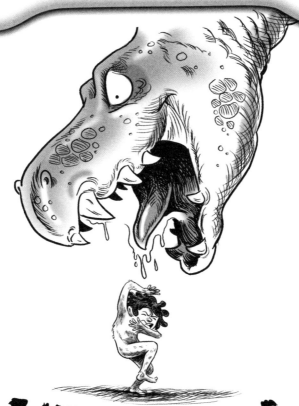

DINOSAUR RESCUE

KYLE MEWBURN & DONOVAN BIXLEY

T-WRECK-ASAURUS

The many moods of Arg's mother

Happy

Angry

Sad

Confused

Scared

Excited

CHAPTER ONE

When Arg told his mum he was going to Slimepot Swamp to collect brontosaurus poo, she frowned. Arg didn't know if it was a good frown or a bad frown. Sometimes it was hard to tell what his mum was thinking. Stone Age people *always* looked like they were frowning. Even when they weren't. And Arg's mum was frownier than most. Arg's dad said that's why he dragged her into his cave ...

But that's another story.

"Swamp bad," she grunted. "Dinosaur eat Arg."

Arg grinned. "Don't worry, Mum. I'll be careful. And Krrk-Krrk will protect me. He can smell danger from a hundred spears away."

Krrk-Krrk gave a small microceratops bark.

Krrk-Krrk was a total scaredy-saur.

But he liked going on adventures.

Arg's mum scratched her head and grunted. Most of the time she didn't understand a word Arg said. One time Arg tried to explain that the reason he was a lot smarter than all the other people in his tribe was because his brain was twice as big as everyone else's. Arg didn't know why he'd been born with such a big brain. He just knew it made him smarter. Heaps smarter.

But Arg's mum had just scratched her armpits and yawned. It was way too complicated for her little brain to understand. She didn't even know what a brain was. She didn't care, either. She didn't like thinking too much. So Arg gave up. Sometimes it was very lonely being so much cleverer than everyone else.

"Big trouble, Arg scream," his mum said. She lifted him up and squeezed him so hard he thought his head would pop.

Arg tried to squirm loose. But his mum was very strong.

"Arg back before sun go," his mum said. "No come, no din-din. Go hungry."

Arg rolled his eyes. That wasn't a punishment, it was more like a reward! The hunting party was still away. All they'd get to eat tonight would be some rotting berries and moss. A roasted cycad root too, if they were lucky. Arg didn't mind missing that. If he caught something yummy to eat at Slimepot Swamp, he'd make sure he was late.

"Yes, Mum," he said.

His mother grunted but didn't put him down.

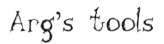

Arg's tools

| Throwy stones | Multi-purpose Swiss Army rock | Pokey poker | Bonger |

She stared at him suspiciously. Then she shoved her finger deep into her nose. When she pulled it out again, there was a big chunk of soft, green snot on the end. She studied it a second before popping it in her mouth.

Arg almost gagged. Sometimes his mum was such a Neanderthal.

As soon as she put him down, Arg ran to his cave.

"Come on, Krrk-Krrk," he said, grabbing his spear and a hollowed storing log. Then off they headed for Slimepot Swamp.

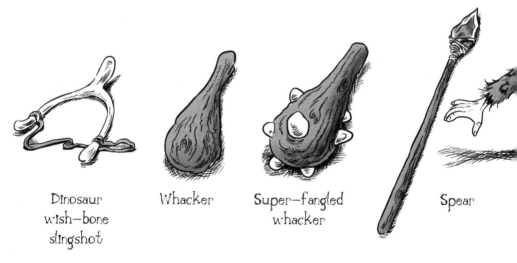

Dinosaur
wish—bone
slingshot

Whacker

Super—fangled
whacker

Spear

A small note about clothes

Nobody in Arg's village wears clothes.
But Arg doesn't like walking around naked.
He didn't mind when he was young, but he's nearly eight summers old now.

Arg's wardrobe

Arg's favourite
sabre—toothed tiger coat

Bear foot slippers
for cold nights

Arg's mum wasn't happy when he started wearing clothes.
"You furry. No need more fur," she grunted.

But Arg wasn't as furry as everyone else. "But, Mu-um," Arg moaned.
"I'm always cold. And the furs keep me warm. I think clothes are a
great idea. Everyone will be wearing them one day."

Arg's mum fished some ear-wax out of her ear and ate it.
"Arg not leave fur lying in cave," she grunted. "Me not brush fur."

Arg's favourite fur is his sabre-toothed tiger coat. Arg ties small fur
bags onto his coats. He sticks his hands in them when it's cold. He can
put other things in them, too. Arg calls the bags 'puckets'. He doesn't
think 'puckets' sounds quite right, but he hasn't come up with a
better name yet.

Turtle shell helmet
for dangerous activities

Puckets
good for
putting cold hands
(and other things) in

Underwear
for hot days

Fresh underwear
in case of accidents

CHAPTER TWO

Pttttthththththththththththth!

The sound of brontosaurus farts echoed across the valley. Pttttthththththththththththth!

Brontosauruses were the biggest farters in the world. Arg thought it was because they ate only vegetables. Arg didn't like vegetables.

All dinosaurs farted. A lot! Cave people farted a lot too. But brontosaurus farts were the hottest, smelliest farts of all. Sometimes Arg worried that all those dinosaur farts would make the world get hotter. He didn't think that would be a good idea because ...

Well, that's another story, too.

Slimepot Swamp was at the end of the valley and was ringed by volcanoes. Rivers of molten lava flowed down all sides. When the lava touched swamp water, it made giant clouds of steam.

FART DANGER TODAY

SSS Just plain stinky
ϾϾ May cause dizziness
O   Will knock you out
X   WARNING! Deadly

The steam was so hot, it could cook you in seconds. The swamp bubbled with sulphur and gurgling mud geysers and there were quicksand pits everywhere.

Slimepot Swamp was not a good place to play.

Arg crept along the edge of the swamp collecting brontosaurus poo. If it was still wet, he squashed it into his hollow log. If it was dry, he put it in his puckets.

He kept glancing up. The brontosaurus herd was in the middle of the swamp. Some of them were eating swamp-grass. Some were wallowing in the mud. Brontosauruses weren't dangerous. But they were very clumsy. It wasn't a good idea to get too close.

The swamp was very noisy. The sound of hissing and farting and brontosaurus roars was deafening. Arg didn't hear the footsteps getting closer. And closer. Then, suddenly …

Screeeeeeeeeeeeech!

The T-rex screech was very loud. And very, VERY close. Arg's ears rang. His heart dropped into his feet. Krrk-Krrk scurried away to hide under a rock. Arg dropped his log and jumped into the swamp. It was his only chance.

He waded towards the brontosauruses. They wouldn't protect him, but the T-rex might decide to eat one of them instead. Arg hoped the T-rex was really hungry and didn't just want a tasty cave-kid snack.

The water smelt awful. Almost as bad as Arg's dad after a hunt.

The mud slurped at Arg's feet. He dragged himself forward. His feet got heavier and heavier. It was like walking through his mum's palm-leaf porridge.

Arg got slower and slower. The water rose to his waist. Arg oozed to a stop. The water rose to his chest.

Arg's eyes grew wide as allosaurus eggs: the water wasn't rising – he was sinking! Quicksand!

Arg knew he was a goner. If the T-rex didn't eat him, the quicksand would swallow him. Arg couldn't decide what was worse. Then he thought of another possibility: the T-rex could chomp him in half, and the quicksand could swallow the rest.

Arg groaned. Sometimes he wished he didn't have such a big brain. It was always thinking up stuff like that.

The T-rex screeched again.

Wait a second, thought Arg. *T-rexes don't screech like that when they're just about to gobble a cave kid.* (And Arg should know. He'd seen lots of cave kids get gobbled by T-rexes. He always thought you had to be stupid to get gobbled by a T-rex. He never imagined he'd get gobbled by a T-rex too. How embarrassing!)

Arg glanced over his shoulder. His face blushed red.

It wasn't a T-rex. It was Shlok. Shlok was an expert at making dinosaur calls. Shlok lifted his

Comparative
brain sizes

Average caveman brain

hands to his mouth. He didn't screech again. This time he howled with laughter.

"Arg jump in swamp!" Shlok hooted. "Shlok scare Arg!"

Shlok was Arg's best friend. He wasn't very smart, but he liked playing practical jokes as much as Arg did. Most of the time they did practical jokes together. But sometimes Shlok got jealous because Arg was so much smarter. Then he'd play a practical joke on Arg.

Arg started to smile. Then he remembered the quicksand.

Shlok's brain

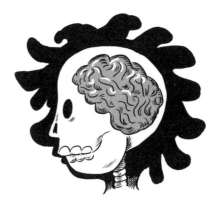

Arg's brain

"Shlok!" he called. "Quick! Get a branch!"
Shlok picked up a stone and threw it at Arg.

"No, a branch!" yelled Arg. The water slurped over his shoulder.

Shlok grunted and disappeared into the jungle. A few seconds later, he returned with a very long branch.

Arg sighed with relief. "Hold it so I can grab it!"

Shlok lifted the branch high above his head …
then threw it. The branch whizzed past Arg's head.

He ducked just in time.

"Don't throw it!" Arg rolled his eyes. "You need to
pull me out!"

Shlok's forehead wrinkled even more than usual.
His jaw jutted forward. It almost hung to his chest.
He was concentrating very hard.

"PULL – ME – OUT!" screamed Arg. He held up his hand. The muddy water gurgled into his ears.

Finally, Shlok understood. He found another branch. It was just long enough. Arg grabbed one end and held on tight. Shlok pulled.

The mud tugged Arg's bottom half. Shlok tugged Arg's top half.

Arg thought he was going to be torn in half.

Then …

Pop!

Shlok hauled Arg free and dragged him to safety.

"Thanks, Shlok." Arg grinned with relief. "That was fun."

Shlok grunted and scratched his bum.

Krrk-Krrk crept out from under the rock. Arg bent down to scratch his ear. He frowned. Krrk-Krrk was still trembling with fear. "It's okay, Krrk-Krrk," said Arg. "It was only Shlok."

A loud T-rex screech sent goosebumps down Arg's furry neck. He shook his head. "You're not going to fool me again, Shlok."

But it wasn't Shlok this time. Shlok was standing upright (well, as upright as he could), listening carefully. The screech came again. It was definitely a T-rex this time. A big one. And it was coming from their village.

30

Arg and Shlok looked at each other. They could tell they were thinking exactly the same thing. All the hunters were away. It was up to them to save their village!

Arg and Shlok sprinted towards their village, their spears swinging at their sides. Arg's knees trembled with fear.

Interesting
facts about
brontosaurus poo

Brontosaurus poo is very useful.

Dry brontosaurus poo can be burnt on the fire. It burns very hot.

It can be used as ammunition for slingshots. It is very hard.

You can suck it like candy. It tastes like liquorice.

YUMMM

Fresh brontosaurus poo is even more useful.

Arg's dad puts fresh brontosaurus poo on the axles of his hunting wagon. It is very greasy.

HUH!

SLIP

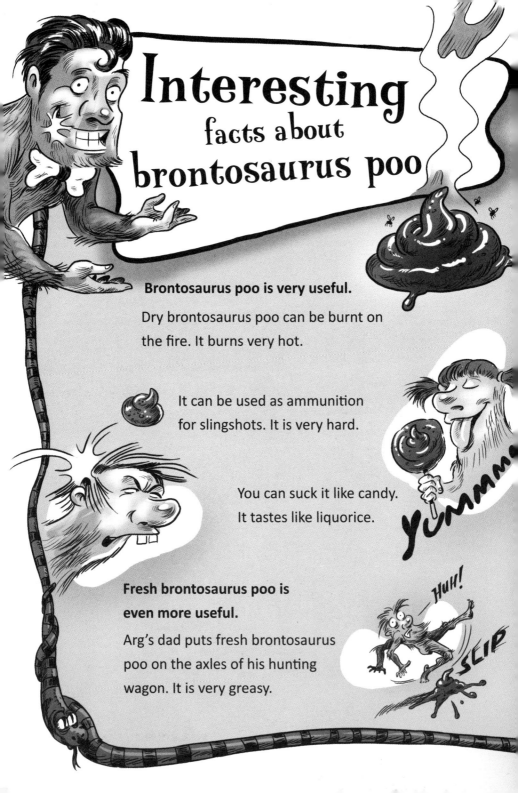

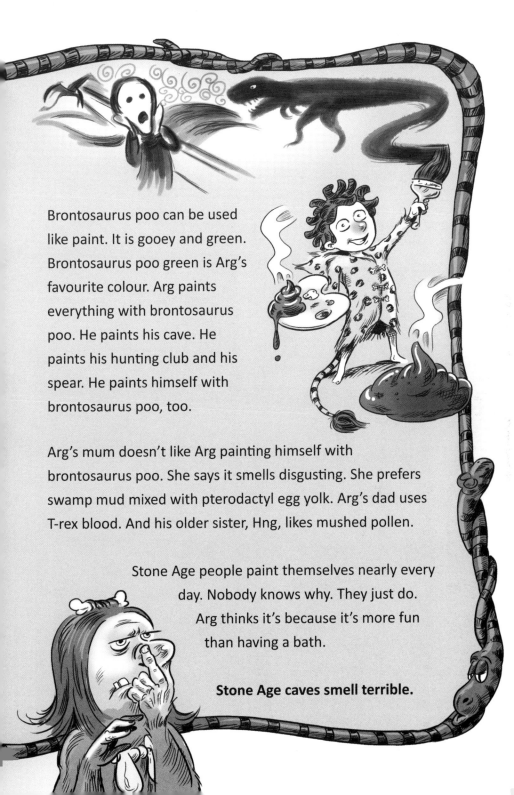

Brontosaurus poo can be used like paint. It is gooey and green. Brontosaurus poo green is Arg's favourite colour. Arg paints everything with brontosaurus poo. He paints his cave. He paints his hunting club and his spear. He paints himself with brontosaurus poo, too.

Arg's mum doesn't like Arg painting himself with brontosaurus poo. She says it smells disgusting. She prefers swamp mud mixed with pterodactyl egg yolk. Arg's dad uses T-rex blood. And his older sister, Hng, likes mushed pollen.

Stone Age people paint themselves nearly every day. Nobody knows why. They just do. Arg thinks it's because it's more fun than having a bath.

Stone Age caves smell terrible.

Arg's family cave

CHAPTER THREE

The track to the village was littered with broken branches and snapped tree trunks. It looked like a hurricane had swept through. But hurricanes didn't leave footprints. Especially not very, very big, T-rex-shaped footprints.

Arg gulped. The T-rex must be massive. And very angry, too.

T-rexes were predators. They were always stalking through the jungle looking for an easy meal. Lucky for cave people, they weren't very good at creeping. You could hear them coming a mile away. However, they didn't normally go around breaking branches or snapping tree trunks. So something must've annoyed this T-rex.

Arg and Shlok ran as fast as they could. Krrk-Krrk ran behind, making fearful whining cries. Arg felt like whining too, but he clenched his teeth instead.

He glanced at Shlok. He couldn't tell what his friend was thinking. Knowing Shlok, he probably wasn't thinking anything at all. He was too dumb to be scared.

They felt the ground trembling. They heard
screams and yells. Then a mighty screech shook
the trees.

Arg and Shlok swapped nervous glances. Shlok's
eyes were watery. His black tongue looked like a
snake, crawling over dry lips. He wasn't too dumb
to be scared after all.

They reached the village clearing. It was a
disaster area.

SWAT

Broken branches were lying everywhere. The bonfire pit was trampled. Half-dried animal hides were hanging in trees. The tribe's flint pile was scattered and shattered and stomped into dust.

Arg looked around. He could see old people and babies huddled at the entrances of their caves. They looked scared. Everyone else was doing their best to scare the T-rex away.

Arg's mum kept charging at the T-rex, swinging a burning stick. Shlok's mum and grandma were throwing rocks down from their cave. All the cave kids were firing stones with their slingshots.

The T-rex was crashing and stumbling in circles. Each time it spun around, its tail sent something – or someone – flying.

Arg scratched his head. Something wasn't quite right.

Before he could figure out what it was, Old Drik
shuffled out of her cave. Old Drik was very old. She
was almost blind and completely deaf. She looked
very angry and shuffled straight towards the T-rex,
wagging her finger.

"Me sleep," she grunted. "Too much bang-bang.
Go away!"

Arg covered his eyes. He couldn't watch.

The T-rex gave a loud screech. Arg waited to hear the sound of crunching bones. Instead, he heard another screech. Then a loud crash.

Arg peered through his fingers. Old Drik was still wagging her finger. But the T-rex wasn't listening. It charged a tree and dragged itself along a branch.

The branch snapped off and crashed to the ground.

The T-rex screeched louder. Then charged the other way. Arg scowled in concentration. It didn't make any sense.

Suddenly, a loud battle call echoed through the clearing. Arg shook his head as Gurg burst out of hiding. Gurg was only two summers older than Arg.

He wasn't strong enough to kill a T-rex. Not by a
long way. But Gurg was too dumb to realise that. He
charged the T-rex, waving his spear.

The T-rex didn't pay any attention. It scraped its
back against the cliff. Rocks and dirt tumbled into
the clearing. A cave baby almost toppled down too.
Its mother caught it just in time.

A big boulder nearly hit Gurg. He leapt over it
and lunged at the T-rex, but his spearhead wasn't
sharp enough to penetrate the dinosaur's tough skin.

Arg rolled his eyes. Gurg was always too lazy to
sharpen his spear.

Gurg wasn't giving up. He shuffled back twenty paces. Then, with a bloodcurdling scream, he charged and threw himself at the T-rex. This time, his spear split open the dinosaur's scaly skin. Blood spurted everywhere.

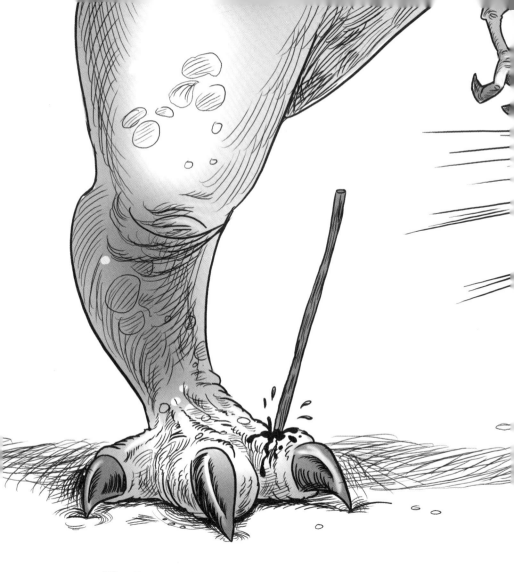

The T-rex jerked as if it had been stung by a bee. Its head spun around. It looked very confused. When it noticed Gurg digging his spear into its foot,

it bent down and ... **CHOMP!**

It chomped Gurg in half and spat him out.

Arg shrugged. He never liked Gurg anyway.

And there were more important things to think
about. Like why the T-rex didn't eat Gurg. T-rexes
never missed a chance for an easy meal.

"Me fight T-rex," grunted Shlok. "Me die like
brave hunter."

You die like stupid cave kid, thought Arg. *Just like Gurg.*

Shlok got ready to charge, but Arg stopped him.

The T-rex threw its tiny arms in the air and spun around again.

"Wait! I've just figured out what's wrong!"
Arg grinned.

T-rexes were ruthless killers. They could kill
with one bite. But this T-rex
wasn't trying to kill
anyone. It wasn't
hungry. It was itchy!
It was trying to
scratch its back, but
its arms were too
short to reach!

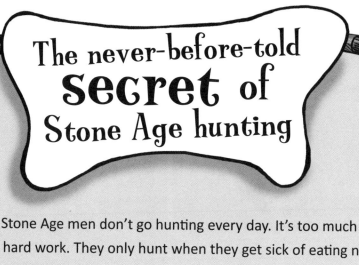

The never-before-told
secret of
Stone Age hunting

Stone Age men don't go hunting every day. It's too much hard work. They only hunt when they get sick of eating nuts and berries.

Hunting trips can take a long time. Dinosaurs aren't very clever, but they're clever enough to know that Stone Age people want to eat them. So they usually stay far away.

Hunters don't hunt big dinosaurs like brontosauruses or T-rexes. Hunters say that's because these dinosaurs are too big to carry. But really it's because they are too dangerous. Hunters like to have fun and show off. They don't like to get squashed or eaten.

Sometimes they only *pretend* to go hunting. Instead of heading for the dinosaur grazing places, they go to a secret place. They drink fermented dinosaur milk and tell stories all day.

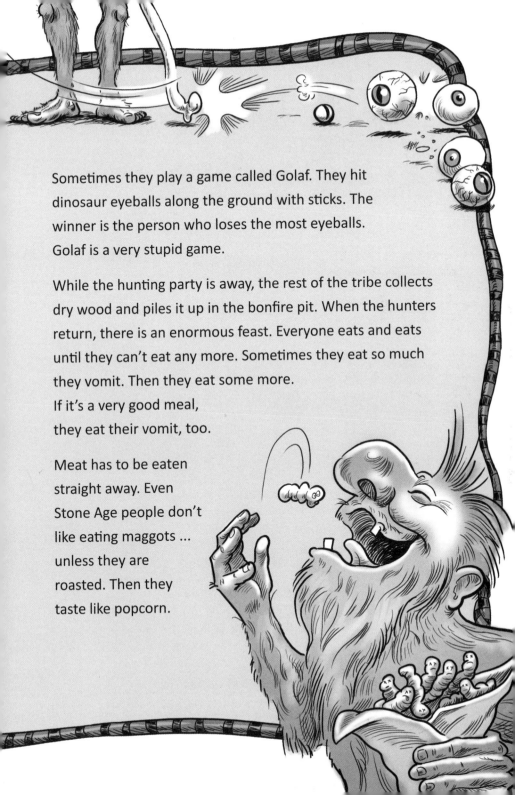

Sometimes they play a game called Golaf. They hit dinosaur eyeballs along the ground with sticks. The winner is the person who loses the most eyeballs. Golaf is a very stupid game.

While the hunting party is away, the rest of the tribe collects dry wood and piles it up in the bonfire pit. When the hunters return, there is an enormous feast. Everyone eats and eats until they can't eat any more. Sometimes they eat so much they vomit. Then they eat some more.
If it's a very good meal,
they eat their vomit, too.

Meat has to be eaten straight away. Even Stone Age people don't like eating maggots ... unless they are roasted. Then they taste like popcorn.

CHAPTER FOUR

Arg had fleas once. They itched and itched. It almost drove him crazy. His mum preened him for hours. She brushed through his light coat, chasing one flea after another. When she caught them, she popped them into her mouth. But there were too many fleas to eat. After a while, she was so full she had to lie down. And Arg was still crawling with fleas.

Arg's mum thought he got the fleas from his sabre-toothed tiger coat. She was always blaming Arg's clothes. But Arg knew exactly where he got them from – his grandad. There were all sorts of creepy-crawly things living on Arg's grandad. That's because he never let anyone preen him.

Arg tried everything to get rid of the fleas. Smoky fires. Cold baths. He even thought about shaving off all his fur with a sharp flint – that's how desperate he was.

Finally, Arg got the idea to lie in a pool of hot mud. What a relief!

He almost felt sorry for the T-rex. But how was he going to get it to lie down in a pool of hot mud? T-rexes didn't like taking orders. Not from anybody. And the nearest hot mud pool was in Slimepot Swamp.

Arg looked around. His tribe were starting to get desperate. They were sure the T-rex was trying to eat them all. All the mums were huddled behind a rock, sharpening their spears.

Arg knew they were

getting ready to charge. If that happened, the T-rex
might forget its itch and attack them. Arg's mum was
a good spear thrower. But it would take a hundred
spears to kill a T-rex. They'd just make it angry. And
an angry T-rex could kill them all!

"We've got to do something," Arg hissed.
He glanced around at Shlok. His stomach
did a somersault.

Shlok must have had the same idea. He was

creeping along the edge of the clearing – inching
closer to the T-rex.

There was no time to lose.

Arg sprinted across the clearing, heading straight
for the T-rex. He hoped he was right about the itch.
If he wasn't ...

The T-rex twisted around. It tried to drag its back
against a broken tree stump but lost its balance and

stumbled backwards. It nearly stepped right on Arg.
Arg dodged and weaved. One foot smashed beside
him. The next whistled past his ear.

Suddenly he was right underneath the T-rex. Its
underbelly was thin and pale. He could see its heart
throbbing just beneath. If he shoved his spear
upwards as hard as he could, he might be able to kill
it. He'd be a hero.

Arg held his spear tightly with both hands and
stared at the throbbing spot. It was an easy target.

The T-rex didn't know he was there. But he had only a few seconds. If he wanted to do it, he had to do it now.

Slowly, he shook his head. He didn't want to be a
hero. And he didn't want to kill the T-rex. It wasn't
smart to kill for no reason. He didn't want the T-rex
to kill any more of his tribe, either. Especially not
Shlok or his mum.

Arg's mum burst out from behind her rock. She
gave a bloodcurdling scream. Arg's older sister, Hng,
didn't move. Arg wasn't sure, but it looked like she
was smiling.

Arg sprinted over to the huge tree in the middle of
the clearing. The branches were far apart. He needed
both hands to climb it, so he dropped his spear and
hauled himself up. Higher and higher.

As soon as Arg's mum saw him climbing to safety, she retreated back behind the rock. Hng scowled in disappointment.

Shlok didn't see Arg clambering up the tree. He thought Arg had been squashed by the T-rex. He gave a mighty growl and charged. Arg yelled, but Shlok couldn't hear a thing above the dinosaur's roar.

Arg stared. He hoped Shlok wasn't as stupid as Gurg. If he tried to spear the T-rex, he'd be crunched, too.

Shlok sprinted closer. The T-rex swung around. When Shlok was close enough, he launched his spear.

It sailed through the air like a rocket...

It whizzed past the T-rex's ear...

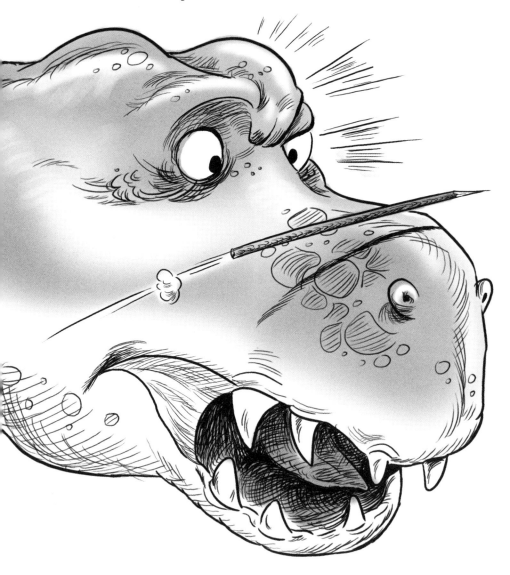

and harpooned into the tree ...

T'HWACK

right beside Arg.

Arg shook his head. Shlok was
such a terrible shot. How could
anyone miss something as big as
a T-rex?

Arg knew it was up to him.
He just had to get to the top of
the tree before Shlok accidentally
speared him.

He tried to climb higher. He couldn't move. The
spear had gone right through his sabre-toothed coat.
He was stuck! He tried to pull the spear out. But it
was buried deep in the trunk. Shlok wasn't a good
aim, but he was very strong.

Arg wriggled and squirmed. He couldn't pull his

coat loose. The sabre-toothed tiger skin was very tough.

There was only one thing Arg could do.

He slipped out of his coat and clambered higher.
His face flushed red with embarrassment. He didn't
feel smart. He felt like a stupid, naked monkey.
And everyone was watching him.

 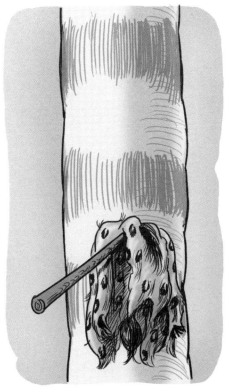

He reached the top branch, then squatted, waiting.

The T-rex danced across the clearing. It slammed against the tree.

Arg took a deep breath, then jumped. He landed on
the T-rex's back. It started to buck wildly. Its head
whipped around. Razor-sharp teeth slashed past
Arg's nose.

Arg held onto its scales with all his strength.
Lucky its arms were too short to reach Arg.

The T-rex's whole back rippled and twitched.
Arg's hands curled into claws.

Arg started to scratch as hard as he could. The T-rex stumbled backwards. It was heading straight for the cliff. Arg was going to get crushed!

Arg slipped down the T-rex's back and scratched harder. The creases in his forehead filled with sweat. His furry legs ached with tiredness.

Then the T-rex gave an ear-shattering screech ... and sighed to a halt.

Arg started to sigh with relief. The
T-rex didn't move. It started to make a
strange purring sound. The sound
vibrated through its whole body,

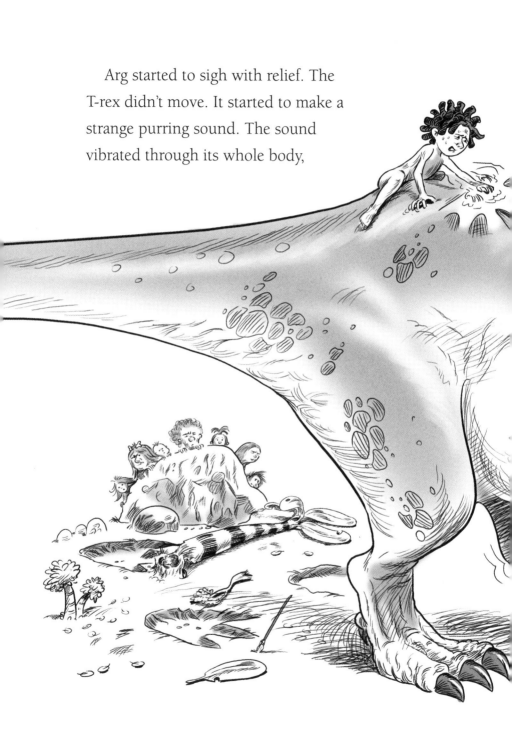

vibrating Arg too. His teeth chattered. His
body trembled. But he kept scratching.
Suddenly, the vibrations stopped.

The T-rex jerked up.

Arg glanced up and groaned. His whole tribe was charging towards them. They were waving spears and clubs and burning sticks, and yelling as loudly as they could.

The T-rex spun one way then the other. Behind it, the cliff rose nearly straight up. A wave of shouting cave people were closing in rapidly on all sides.

It was outnumbered; trapped.

It screeched fiercely, then charged. Arg's mum dived out of the way. Spears rained down all around. The T-rex broke through. It didn't pause when it reached the edge of the clearing; it crashed through the wall of creepers and moss and disappeared into the jungle.

Arg clung tightly to its back, screaming all the way.

CHAPTER FIVE

The T-rex didn't sidestep around bushes. It didn't
dodge around volcanic boulders. It didn't change
course for anything. It crashed through the jungle
like a giant unstoppable tank.

THWACK

Branches whipped Arg's face. Vines swung down and tried to strangle him. But he held on.

T-rexes could run very fast. Everything whizzed past. Arg couldn't tell which way they were going. If the T-rex ran too far, Arg would never find his way back to the clearing. He'd be left all alone in a dark, scary jungle full of boy-eating dinosaurs.

Lost forever ... or at least until he got eaten. No dinosaur would care how big Arg's brain was.

They plunged out of the jungle into a small, swampy clearing. A tall cliff blocked their way. Arg looked up … and up … and up. He couldn't see the top. It disappeared into the sky. The T-rex didn't turn. It didn't slow down. It ran as fast as it could. It splashed through the swamp – heading straight for the cliff.

They were going to crash!

Arg closed his eyes.
He couldn't watch.
This was going to hurt.
He counted silently
on his fingers.

One …

two …

The sound of the jungle faded. The only things Arg could hear were the T-rex's heavy breathing and his own pounding heart. Everything was echoing. That was strange.

Arg slowly opened one eye ...

The other eye sprang open too.

He blinked both eyes. They were definitely open but he couldn't see a thing! Was he blind from fright? No … he could see a faint light ahead. It was getting brighter. They must be in a tunnel.

Suddenly they burst into light. The T-rex slowed
to a standstill and stood, puffing heavily.

Arg looked around. There was no jungle on this
side of the tunnel. No swamps or bubbling geysers,

either. There were rolling green fields dotted with
wildflowers as far as he could see. It wasn't at all
scary like the jungle. It looked kind of friendly even.

The fields were full of dinosaurs, too. Dinosaurs of

every kind. They weren't screeching and roaring
at each other. They were hardly even farting.
They were grazing peacefully, side by side.
The valley was so peaceful, Arg could hear

a river chuckling over rocks.

A raptor lumbered towards them.

That meant trouble!

Arg leapt off the T-rex's back into the branches of a nearby tree.

Bad move. The raptor spotted Arg and stomped towards him.

The T-rex lumbered to block it. It screeched loudly and bared its fangs. The raptor scurried away.

Arg scrambled higher as the T-rex leant closer. Arg smelt its bad breath. Its teeth gleamed in its very big mouth.

"You can't eat me!" gulped Arg. His mouth felt like it was full of fur. "I helped you!"

The T-rex blinked. "What did you just say?"

Arg's mouth gaped open. Did the T-rex just speak?

"I was saying it wouldn't be fair to eat me," he said.

"You can talk!" said the T-rex.

"Of course I can talk," grumbled Arg. "I'm not stupid."

"No, indeed," chuckled the T-rex as he studied Arg from every angle. "Hmmmm. Has your brain *always* been that big?"

"No, I found it under a cycad," said Arg, rolling his eyes. "DUH!"

The T-rex almost blushed. "Sorry. Stupid question, I know. I guess I'm not really used to talking to other clever creatures."

"Can all dinosaurs talk?" asked Arg.

The T-rex laughed. "No. Lucky for me! I'd feel terrible eating prey that was saying 'please don't eat me'." The T-rex laughed until he stopped.

"Sorry about your friend, by the way," the T-rex said. He grimaced with embarrassment. "I didn't mean to chomp him. But he was just *so* annoying. Poking my foot with his spear like that. It really hurt."

Arg shrugged. "That's all right. He's not my friend anyway."

Arg had a million questions but there wasn't time for a single one.

The T-rex sprang to attention. "Oh dear, I better get you back home before someone tracks you here. Quick, jump on my back!"

The T-rex dropped Arg in the jungle beside the clearing. Arg could hear his mum performing a death wail. She was very upset. She thought he must be dead.

The T-rex started to leave.

"What's your name?" asked Arg.

The T-rex frowned. "My name?'

"You know. What your family and your friends call you," said Arg.

"I don't have any family. Or friends," sighed the T-rex.

"My name's Arg." Arg held out his hand. The T-rex shook it. "I think I'll call you Skeet ... if you don't mind."

93

Skeet T-Wreck-asaurus

1. Massive jaws for chomping prey
2. Huge teeth – up to 23cm long
3. Pathetic little arms – useless for just about everything
4. Powerful legs – can run at 25km per hour
5. Absolutely ginormous brain. Note that it is 10 times the size of a normal dinosaur brain!
6. Long tail – counterbalances the weight of the head

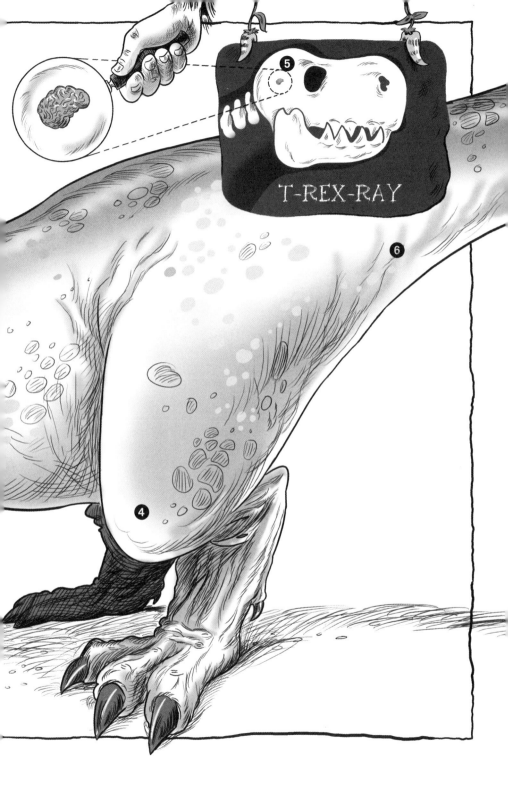

The T-rex thought about that. Then he smiled. "No, Arg, I don't mind at all."

"What were you doing in our valley, Skeet?" Arg suddenly asked. If Arg lived in a friendly valley like Skeet's, he'd never set foot outside. It was way too dangerous.

Skeet gave Arg a long, sad look. Then he sighed. It was a very long sigh. Very smelly, too. Arg held his breath and waited.

"When I was growing up, there used to be dinosaurs everywhere. But every year there are fewer and fewer."

Arg nodded. "That's what my dad says."

Skeet sighed again. "When I found the secret valley, I knew I had to try and rescue as many of us as I could. Before we all become extinct. But it's very hard work. Dangerous, too. Dinosaurs can be very stubborn. And stupid."

"So can humans," said Arg. He started sighing, too. But stopped halfway as another brilliant idea exploded in his huge brain. "Maybe I could help!"

Skeet chuckled. "What a great idea!" He gave Arg a big wink. "Us clever creatures should stick together, eh? See you later, Arg."

Arg's smile was wide as a half-moon as he pushed through the last curtain of creepers. He might be the only human with a big brain but somehow he didn't feel so lonely any more.

He sprinted across the clearing, hooting and hollering all the way.

"Aaaaaahh . . ."

Arg was in the middle of a lovely dream when a
fierce growl rumbled through the cave. Arg's reflexes
catapulted him off his bedrock before he was even
awake. He snatched up his spear and spun around to
face the intruder.

He expected to see a sabre-toothed tiger chewing
on his sister Hng. (Actually, that's what he was *hoping*
he'd see. Just like in his lovely dream. He dreamt
something ate his sister nearly every night. Some
nights he dreamt that she got melted by lava or
swallowed by a geyser. Those were nice dreams, too.
But the sabre-toothed tiger dream was his favourite.)

But it wasn't a sabre-toothed tiger. Or a hungry raptor. Or even a Grogllgrox raiding party. It was something much, *much* worse.

"... CHOOOOOoo!"

Arg's dad let out an enormous sneeze. A spray of thick green snot rocketed across the cave like a meteor shower. There was no time to duck. Arg had just enough time to close his mouth.

splat!

A huge glob of snot splattered
into Arg's right cheek. More globs hit
the cave wall. A massive glob got caught in one of
the spider webs draped across the cave roof.

It swung like a snotty stalagtite for a few seconds,

then dropped on top of Arg's head.

"Ugh, Dad!" groaned Arg, wiping the snot from his face. It was light green with chunks of yellow in it. It stuck to his hand like cycad sap and he couldn't resist sniffing it. "Pooh! That's disgusting!"

He rubbed his hand roughly along his cloak. The snot left a stinky smear across the fur. At least he was wearing clothes. Imagine if he ran around half naked like the rest of his tribe! The thought made him shudder.

When his hand was sort of clean, he combed his fingers through his hair. The snot was still warm. He got out as much as he could, then cleaned his hand in the dirt. Arg's hair was stiff with snot. It stood up like a Triceratops horn.

"Dad!" Arg scolded. "Can't you cover your mouth and nose when you sneeze?"

Arg's dad pointed at Arg and laughed. "Arg funny."

Arg's dad was sitting on the cave floor with a fresh mammoth hide draped over his shoulders. A *very* fresh mammoth hide. He'd caught it less than two moons ago. There were still bits of meat and blood stuck to it and it was starting to smell. But Arg's dad didn't notice.

Arg rolled his eyes. Sometimes his dad was such a Neanderthal.

Arg looked around the family cave. On second thoughts, his entire family were Neanderthals. The floor was littered with bones and chunks of meat, which were crawling with maggots. There was a big pile of rotting cycad roots in one corner.

In the opposite corner was a big pile of ... something.
Arg didn't want to know what *that* was. It was
buzzing with flies and smelt worse than his dad.

Arg's dad started to sneeze again.

"Ah–ah–ahh ..."

Arg took a step. Something cold
and squelchy oozed between his
toes but there was no time to
wonder what it was. He hurried to his dad.

"Cover your mouth, Dad," said Arg. "Like this."
He held his hand in front of his mouth and nose like
a shield. "See?"

For a second, Arg thought his dad understood.
Then Arg's dad snatched Arg's hand and stuck it in
front of his own mouth.

"Not *my* hand," Arg yelped. He tried to pull his
hand away but his dad was too strong. Arg felt a rush
of hot breath. Then …

"–choo!"

Arg's hand was blasted with hot, stinky snot. It felt
like he'd stuck his hand up a dead pterodactyl's bum
– except a million times worse. Arg should know,
too. The youngest hunter was always the one who
had to stick his hand up dead pterodactyls' bums to
check for eggs. Once Arg even stuck his hand up a
live pterodactyl's bum …

But that's another story.

How to collect pterodactyl eggs

1. Make sure it's dead

2. Grab it firmly by the tail

3. Grease up
your hand with
brontosaurus poo

4. Insert hand ...

5. Hey presto!

Arg's dad started to laugh. It turned into a fierce cough. He let go of Arg's hand and flopped back onto the floor.

"Me sick," groaned Arg's dad. "No hunt."

Arg's jaw dropped to his chest. For a few seconds he looked like a normal cave boy. Then his brain started working again. His dad had to be terribly sick not to go hunting. He needed help. Fast.

"Don't worry, Dad. I'll get Mum," said Arg.
"Come on, Krrk-Krrk."

Krrk-Krrk didn't follow. He was too busy licking
something yummy off the floor.

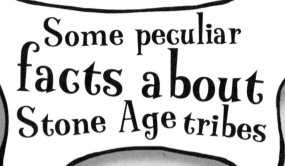

Some peculiar facts about Stone Age tribes

Stone age tribes are like big families. Everyone in the tribe is related to each other somehow. Like Arg's dad is also Shlok's uncle. And Shlok is Arg's mum's brother. Which kind of makes Shlok Arg's uncle as well as his best friend. And Arg's sister Hng is ... well, it's way too confusing to think about it. Even for someone with a big brain like Arg.

The best way to tell if someone is from your tribe is to smell their armpits. If they are from your tribe, they will smell just like you. At least that's what Arg's dad told him. Arg asked how he knew what people

Sniff
Sniff

from other tribes smelt like under their arms. But his dad just got all embarrassed and didn't explain. Arg's not sure if he believes it but he doesn't really want to find out.

Most tribes don't like to fight. Usually they try to avoid each other. If they see another tribe coming, they will hide. If there's no good place to hide, they will act tough. They will call each other names – like geyser-face, or volcano-breath.

Sometimes they throw things at each other. Like rocks or rotten iguanodon eggs or brontosaurus poo. They keep acting tough until they get hungry. Then they stop. Acting tough is hard work.

The only tribe that likes to fight are the Grogllgrox. They are very bloodthirsty. If they catch you, they will cut off the top of your head and eat your brains. Sometimes they don't even kill you first. Nobody likes the Grogllgrox. Not even other Grogllgrox.

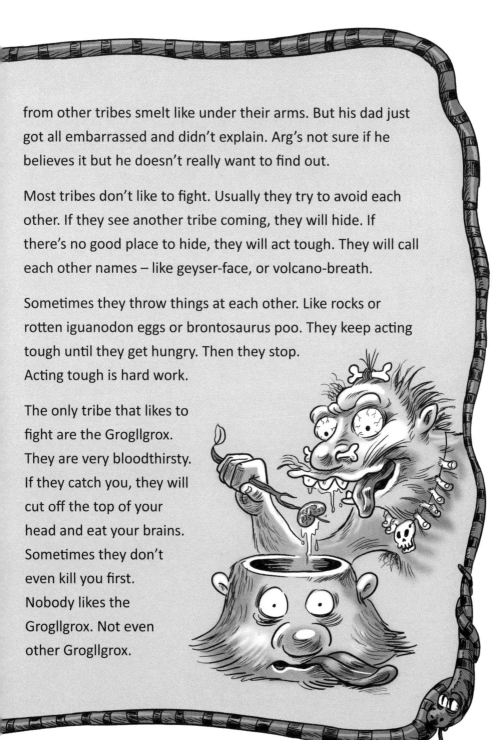

CHAPTER TWO

Arg raced outside yelling, "Mum! Mum!"

He expected to find her beside the fire pit making breakfast. Or at the flint pile, sharpening new flints for his dad's spears. Or folding bits of charred meat inside leaves for his dad to take along on his hunting expedition in case he got hungry.

But there was no sign of his mum. And no reply. That was weird. His mum never went far from the family cave, except when all the women went on gathering expeditions.

Actually, that wasn't totally true. Stone age women weren't *supposed* to go too far from the family cave. But Arg's mum never did what she was supposed to do. She often sneaked away on secret adventures.

Sometimes she went to Slimepot Swamp to roll in the bubbling mud. She said that's what made her look so beautiful. Arg thought it just made her smell bad. But mostly she went to collect special ingredients to make powerful medicines.

His mum was always inventing medicine to make people get better.

Once, Arg tried to follow her. She was very angry when she caught him. "Medicine secret woman work," she'd told him. "No work if man see. Arg not follow."

Arg didn't like his mum sneaking off by herself. There were lots of dangerous predators in the valley. Not to mention Grogllgrox. But he was too scared of his mum to disobey her.

Hng was sitting beside the fire pit, busy squashing fire ants with her thumb. She didn't look up when Arg rushed outside.

"Have you seen Mum?" Arg asked. He didn't really expect Hng to tell him even if she knew. But he was desperate.

Hng slowly looked up. "Mum go."

"Where Mum go?" asked Arg.

He rolled his eyes dramatically. Talking to Hng was as much fun as talking to a trilobite. Just about as interesting, too.

120

Hng's lips curled into a smile. It wasn't a nice smile. She looked like a demented chimpanzee.

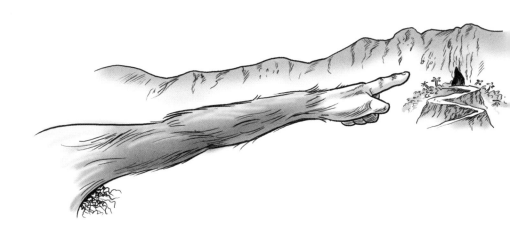

Hng slowly lifted one dirty finger and pointed along
the valley rim. Her forehead was creased in
concentration. When her finger finally stopped,
it was pointing at a large cave at the top of the cliff
on the far side of the valley.

Arg stared at her suspiciously. "Why would Mum
go all the way up there?"

Hng stared back. For a second, she looked almost
intelligent. Then she shrugged, and went back to
squashing fire ants.

Arg didn't trust her at all. Sometimes he wondered if
Hng was really his sister. She was so nasty, she could
be a Grogllgrox. There was only one way to find out …
but Arg would rather stick his hand up a pterodactyl's
bottom than sniff Hng's armpits. That's for sure!

Arg felt something scaly scrape against his leg and looked down. It was Krrk-Krrk. Arg thought he was being friendly ... until he saw a glob of green, slimy snot stuck to the top of Krrk-Krrk's head.

Krrk-Krrk wasn't being friendly. He was trying to rub the snot off onto Arg's leg!

"Urgh!" said Arg. He shoved Krrk-Krrk away with his foot. Krrk-Krrk flipped over and squirmed in the dirt. But he jumped to his feet when Arg sprinted off across the valley.

Arg was covered in sweat and squashed mosquitos by the time he reached the opposite side. That was the worst thing about not being as hairy as everyone else – the mosquitos loved him. They followed him everywhere.

Actual size of a prehistoric mosquito

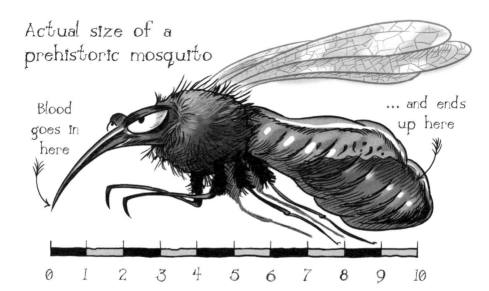

Blood goes in here

... and ends up here

0   1   2   3   4   5   6   7   8   9   10

"Mum!" Arg called as loud as he could. "Mum!"

He craned his neck. A narrow path wound its way up the cliff to the cave. Arg scratched his head. Why would his mum go all the way up there? He racked his brains. The only reason he could think of was that she was collecting some special ingredient for a powerful medicine to make Arg's dad better. But why didn't she answer?

There was only one way to find out.

The gruesome truth about Stone Age medicine

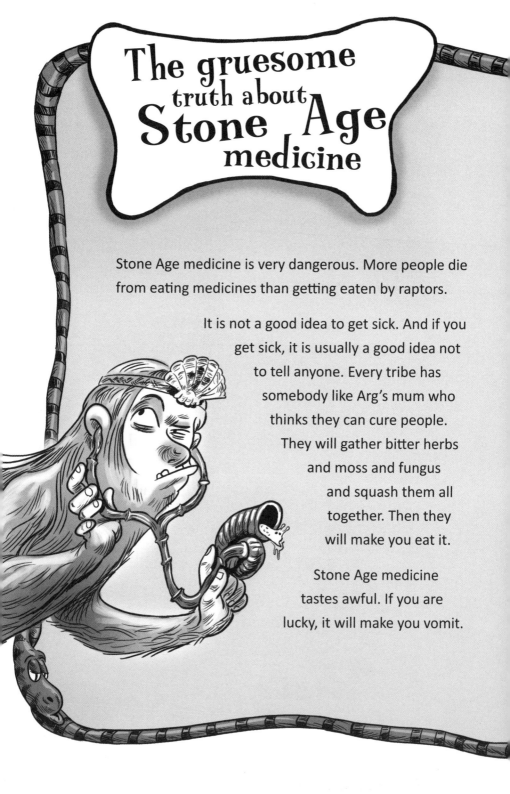

Stone Age medicine is very dangerous. More people die from eating medicines than getting eaten by raptors.

It is not a good idea to get sick. And if you get sick, it is usually a good idea not to tell anyone. Every tribe has somebody like Arg's mum who thinks they can cure people. They will gather bitter herbs and moss and fungus and squash them all together. Then they will make you eat it.

Stone Age medicine tastes awful. If you are lucky, it will make you vomit.

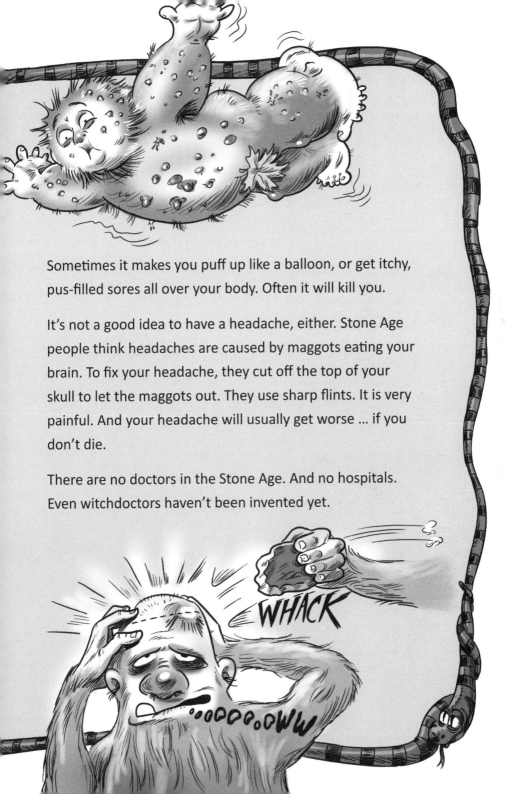

Sometimes it makes you puff up like a balloon, or get itchy, pus-filled sores all over your body. Often it will kill you.

It's not a good idea to have a headache, either. Stone Age people think headaches are caused by maggots eating your brain. To fix your headache, they cut off the top of your skull to let the maggots out. They use sharp flints. It is very painful. And your headache will usually get worse ... if you don't die.

There are no doctors in the Stone Age. And no hospitals. Even witchdoctors haven't been invented yet.

WHACK

ooOOO0.oWW

CHAPTER THREE

The cliff was steep and rocky. Every time Arg swatted at an annoying mosquito, his foot slipped off the path and a mini avalanche went crashing down into the valley. Krrk-Krrk trailed far behind, yapping wildly.

Arg finally reached the cave. It was very big – and very, very dark.

"Mum!" Arg yelled. His voice charged into the cave. A second later it scuttled back out as an echo. Arg's feet stayed glued to the spot. He listened closely. He heard something scratching. Then a loud fart. It was followed by a soft groan. It *sounded* like his mum ... sort of.

"Mum? Are you in there?"

The groaning got louder. If it *was* his mum, she might be hurt. That thought got Arg's feet moving.

He inched forward. One hand slid along the wall so he wouldn't lose direction. The other hand gripped his spear tightly. The walls were damp and

slimy. But they weren't as damp and slimy as the palms of Arg's hands. After ten steps, his shadow got swallowed by the darkness.

The groaning stopped. The cave was cold and silent, except for a faint dripping sound. He took another step. Then froze.

What was that noise? For a few seconds, all he could hear was his own heart pounding in his chest. Then another sound barged into his ears. It sounded like breathing. Heavy breathing.

Suddenly Krrk-Krrk yelped. Arg glanced over his shoulder. Krrk-Krrk was standing at the cave mouth. He was yelping furiously and spinning in circles. That could mean only one thing.

A low, throaty growl spun Arg back. As his pupils widened, a darker shape separated from the blackness. Two flaming red eyes appeared, bobbing in the darkness high above Arg's head.

"Mum?" he squeaked.

Arg didn't know what it was. But it definitely wasn't his mum. It sounded big. Very big. The growling got louder. Arg could hear the creature licking its lips. It sounded very hungry.

Arg backed away. He didn't dare turn round. That was the first lesson Arg's dad ever taught him about hunting. Don't turn your back on your prey.

But what were you supposed to do if you *were* the prey?

Arg's shadow reappeared on the floor. It made him feel a bit less lonely but it didn't make him any less afraid. At least he knew there wasn't much cave left to go. The entrance couldn't be far now. If he ran as fast as he could, he might just escape. It all depended on how fast the thing stalking towards him was.

Arg backed into sunshine.

A second later a massive furry beast stomped into the light. Arg's heart sank. It was a cave bear. Cave bears were the most ferocious killers in the valley. Worse than raptors. The bear opened its mouth. Its huge fangs sparkled with drool.

Some people said if you got attacked by a cave bear you should play dead. Arg wasn't planning on finding out if that were true. He twisted round and dived out of the cave mouth.

The bear's roar made the whole cave tremble.

As Arg's foot hit the path,
a rock came loose. He lost his
balance and toppled over the edge.
At least the bear can't catch me now, he thought as
he rumbled down the rocky slope like a runaway log.

But he was wrong.

The bear wasn't going to miss out on an easy snack. It leapt over the edge and slid down the hill after Arg. Its massive paws kicked up a tornado of dust and debris.

Arg screamed. The bear roared.

CRASH!

Arg smashed into the valley floor.

He felt as if every bone
in his body was broken,
but he managed to clamber
to his feet just as the bear slid
to a halt beside him.

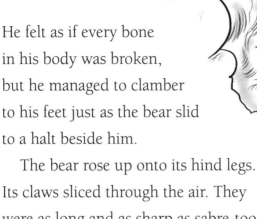

The bear rose up onto its hind legs.
Its claws sliced through the air. They
were as long and as sharp as sabre-toothed
tiger teeth. Arg ducked as they whizzed
past his neck. He backed away, glancing wildly
around. Where was his spear? He didn't want to
die without a fight.

The bear's jaws gaped open. Its breath smelt
disgusting. Thick strings of drool hung from its
fangs. Arg scrunched up his eyes and waited
to be chomped in half.

"Screeeeeeeeeeeech!"

The T-rex screech was very loud. And very close.

Arg's eyes sprang open. It sounded like Skeet. He was saved! Arg's head whipped around ... then he let out a loud groan. It wasn't Skeet.

It was Shlok.

"Bear go!" yelled Shlok, waving his spear.
He marched closer.

Arg wasn't sure if Shlok was very brave. Or very
stupid. Or both.

The bear licked its lips. It stepped closer.
Its shadow blocked out the sun.

"Run, Shlok!" yelled Arg.
They didn't both have to die.
"Run!"

"Go! Bear go!" grunted Shlok, shaking his fist.

Suddenly the bear let out a fierce growl, then dropped onto all fours. Arg thought it was going to charge. He was very surprised when it swung away and lumbered down the valley.

"Woo-hoo-hoo!" howled Shlok. "Shlok scare bear! Shlok brave hunter!" He started dancing around in a circle, hooting with happiness.

Arg couldn't believe his eyes. Why would a cave bear be afraid of Shlok? It didn't make sense. They should both be dead by now.

He saw the answer over Shlok's shoulder. Skeet was standing on the jungle edge, waving his tiny arms wildly. No wonder the bear got scared. Not even a cave bear was going to mess with a T-rex.

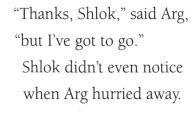

"Thanks, Shlok," said Arg, "but I've got to go."

Shlok didn't even notice when Arg hurried away.

142

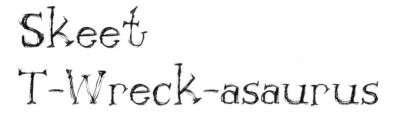

Skeet T-Wreck-asaurus

1. Nostrils and huge sinus cavities – for producing masses of snot
2. Huge teeth – up to 23cm long
3. Pathetic little arms – useless for just about everything, especially wiping a runny nose
4. Powerful legs – can run at 25km per hour
5. Absolutely ginormous brain. Note that it is 10 times the size of a normal dinosaur brain!
6. Long tail – counterbalances the weight of snot-filled head

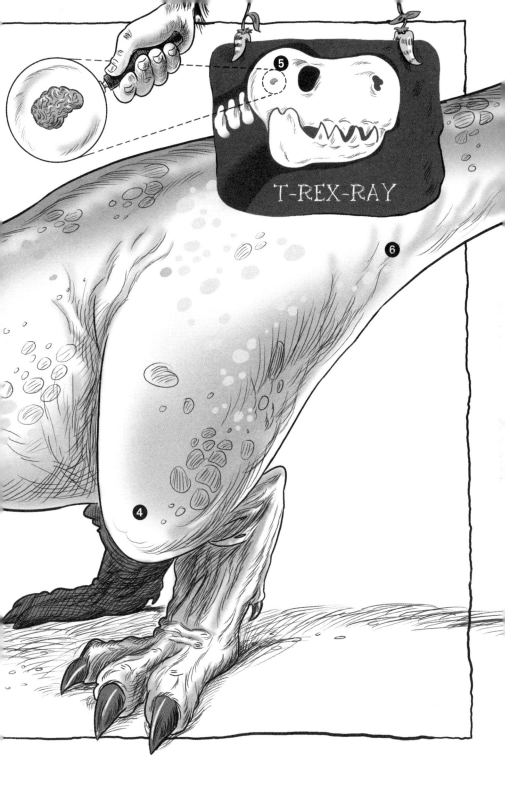

T-REX-RAY

CHAPTER FOUR

When Arg first met Skeet, he was very excited to discover that Skeet had a big brain too. (Actually, that wasn't completely true. When he *first* met Skeet, he was terrified. T-rexes were ferocious killers who ate anything that moved. They didn't care how big your brain was. It was only when Skeet started talking that Arg realised Skeet wasn't going to eat him after all. That's when he started getting excited.)

He was even *more* excited when Skeet asked Arg to help rescue the dinosaurs from extinction. It got very boring hanging around Neanderthals all the time. All they wanted to talk about was eating and hunting. They weren't very good at games, either.

Like the time Arg made up a game called Me See.

The rules were very simple. "I'll think of something and tell you what sound it starts with," Arg explained to Shlok, "then you try to guess what it is. Ready?"

Shlok hoisted his foot to his mouth and started gnawing on a long, dirty toenail.

"Me see something starting with 'tr'," said Arg. "Now you guess."

Shlok spat out his toenail and slowly looked around ... and around ... and around ...

"Just guess," said Arg. "It's an easy one."

"Rock," said Shlok.

Arg rolled his eyes. "Rock starts with 'rr', not 'tr'."

"Rock!" Shlok repeated. He picked up a large rock and smiled as if it were a rotten pterodactyl egg.

UHHHH

Other popular Neanderthal games

UMMMM... What me do?

Early chess

Shlok loved eating rotten pterodactyl eggs. They made the stinkiest farts ever.

"I said something starting with 'tr'," said Arg.

"Rock!" Shlok shouted as he sent the rock hurtling across the clearing. It whizzed past Old Drik's head and shattered against the cliff. "Rock!"

Arg sighed. If Shlok couldn't even guess 'tree', Arg's game was never going to catch on.

Arg hadn't seen Skeet for two moons. But it felt a lot longer. Being the only boy with a big brain was very lonely sometimes. A couple of times, Arg thought

Paper, Scissors, Rock
(but paper and scissors won't be
invented for another million years)

Egg and stick race
(spoons haven't been
invented yet either)

about sneaking off to the secret valley. But he couldn't risk leaving a trail. If a Grogllgrox hunting party found the valley, they'd kill every dinosaur there. Just for fun. Besides, he wasn't sure he could find the valley by himself. That was the problem with secret valleys.

Arg didn't realise just how much he missed Skeet until he saw him standing there. Arg felt like giving him a hug. But how do you hug a T-rex? He couldn't even shake Skeet's hand. Skeet's arms were too short to reach to the ground. And Arg would need a ladder to reach.

"What's wrong, Skeet?" asked Arg. Skeet's nose and eyes were as red as molten lava and there were thick globs of green stuff in the corners of his eyes. He looked terrible. Even for a T-rex.

Sniffle. Snortle. Ah-ah-ahh … *screeeech*!

"I've got people flu," sniffed Skeet. "It's very contagious. Lots of dinosaurs are getting sick. One old brachiosaurus even died."

"That's terrible!" said Arg.

"Indeed," Skeet agreed sadly. "I haven't been back to the secret valley since I started to sniffle. I can't risk spreading it."

Arg slowly nodded his head. If people flu got into the secret valley, all the dinosaurs could become extinct. That would be a disaster!

"Can I help?" he asked.

150

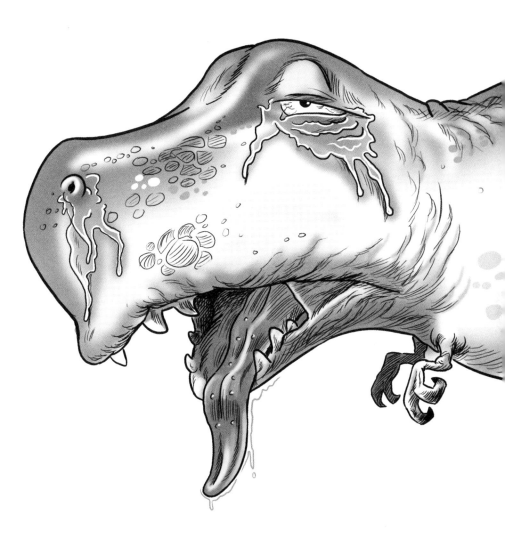

Skeet glanced one way. Then the other.

"Well, there is *one* way you might help," mumbled Skeet. His face turned pink. "But it's kind of ... um ... d—"

"Dangerous?" suggested Arg.

Skeet shook his head. "Nooo, not exactly *dangerous* ..."

"Difficult?"

"Noooooo," said Skeet.

"Daunting? Diabolical? Death-defying?" said Arg.

Skeet rolled his eyes. "Now you're just showing off."

"Just tell me what it is," said Arg, "and I'll do it."

"Are you sure?" asked Skeet.

"I'm sure."

"You promise?"

Arg huffed with frustration. "I promise."

Skeet's teeth widened into a massive grin. "Delightful!"

By the time Skeet finished explaining his plan, Arg
knew the perfect word to describe it: *disgusting*.

Common dinosaur illnesses

Pterosaur
with tears in
his wings

Triceratops
with droopy horns
(very trying)

ITCH ITCH

Ichthyosaurus
with megaladon mumps
(unbearably itchy)

Styracosaurus
with a racking cough

Brontosaurus
with a sore throat
(knot very nice)

Ankylosaurus
with swollen ankles

Arg and Skeet hid on the edge of the jungle beside the Stinkooze Pit. The air was thick with stinky fumes. Everywhere they looked, there were rivers of sticky, stinky, black ooze. It oozed out of the ground. It oozed out of the rocks. Then it all dribbled and drooled into a dark, smelly pit. That's why it was called the Stinkooze Pit.

Everybody stayed far away from the Stinkooze Pit. Even dinosaurs. If a single drop of ooze splattered you, you'd stink for weeks. Nobody would come

near you. Not even your
mum. You'd get kicked
out of your cave and
have to sleep under
a rock.

"They're not here,"
whispered Arg. The smell
was already making him feel
sick. "Maybe we should come
back another day."

"Shhhhhh!" hissed Skeet. "They're coming."

On the other side of the Stinkooze Pit, the jungle parted. One stegosaurus head poked through. Then another. Then several more. When they were sure

the coast was clear, they lumbered into the clearing.

Arg's stomach churned and a bitter taste bubbled up into his mouth. It wasn't the smell. Or even the fact that they were the sickliest stegosauruses Arg

LICK LICK LICK

had ever seen. But their snouts were covered in thick, green snot. Yellow pus oozed from their ears and their eyes were rimmed with gooey gunk.

It was the sight of them licking each other's snotty, gunky faces with long, slimy tongues that turned Arg's stomach.

"Urrrrgggghhh!" groaned Arg. "That's gross!"

"I know," said Skeet, scrunching up his face. "But this is the only herd in the whole valley that hasn't got the really bad sort of people flu. I reckon it's because their snot is like a medicine ... or something."

Arg gave Skeet a long, suspicious look.

"Well, have you got a better idea?" asked Skeet.

Arg's forehead crinkled in concentration. There had to be a better way to save the dinosaurs than this. There just *had* to be! But no matter how hard Arg tried, he couldn't think of a single one.

He let out an enormous sigh. "No."

"I'd do it myself if my arms weren't so short,"
said Skeet.

Arg squared his shoulders until he was standing
nearly upright. It was all up to him. "How much snot
do we need?"

Skeet shrugged. "As much as you can carry,
I guess."

Why the Olympic Games were not invented by Neanderthals

People love to fight, but most people don't like getting killed. That's why sport was invented. Sport is organised fighting – with fancy outfits. The biggest sporting event is the Olympic Games. It's like a war, except nobody gets hurt, and there are lots more ads.

Even though Neanderthals loved to fight, they did *not* invent the Olympic Games, because:

1. Neanderthals are lazy

Organising an Olympic Games is a lot of work. Way too much work for a Neanderthal. They'd much prefer to sit in the shade picking fleas off each other than organise a major sporting event. They wouldn't even go hunting if they didn't get hungry. If Neanderthals had invented the telephone and pizzas, they would never have moved at all.

2. Neanderthals are not very good at following rules

Without rules, most sports wouldn't make sense. Nobody would want to watch a bunch of people running around willy-nilly, or chasing a ball all over the place. If a Neanderthal started running, he might never come back. And he would probably try to eat the ball.

3. Neanderthals don't know how to melt gold (or silver or bronze)

Nobody would bother competing at the Olympic Games if all they won was a rock. Neanderthals don't know how to melt gold (or silver or bronze) to make shiny medals. They don't even know what gold is. The Bronze Age doesn't even start for ages yet.

7. Neanderthals can't count

There's a lot of counting at an Olympic Games. Someone has to count the competitors and make sure each team has the right number of players. Someone has to keep track of the scores and the times. And, at the end, someone has to add all the numbers together to find a winner. It's very complicated. That's why the Olympics were invented by the Ancient Greeks and not Neanderthals. The Ancient Greeks were very good at counting.

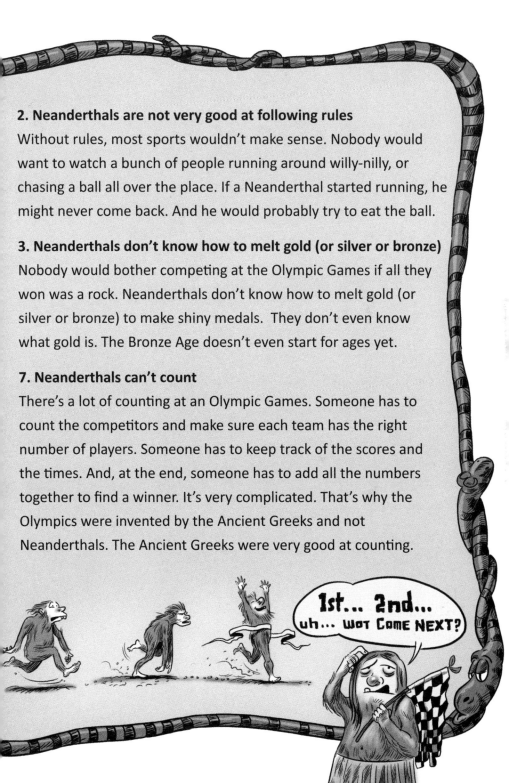

1st... 2nd... uh... WOT COME NEXT?

CHAPTER FIVE

Arg tiptoed around the edge of the
Stinkooze Pit. He wasn't worried about
frightening the stegosauruses. They
had very bad eyesight, and there was
no way they'd smell him with their
snouts full of snot. They didn't
even mind the awful stink
hanging in the air.

But Arg was terrified of
stepping in some ooze.
He liked sleeping on his
own bed-rock. He didn't
want to sleep outside for a
whole moon cycle. It was lonely

enough being the only boy with a big brain. The last thing he needed was to be a smelly outcast, too.

Arg reached the clearing. The stegosauruses were happily grazing on ferns and mosses along the edge of the pit. They didn't notice Arg creeping closer.

The biggest stegosaurus was munching its way right towards Arg. The plates on its back stood up like two rows of giant spearheads. A huge glob of dried snot plugged its right nostril. It was at least twice as big as Arg's head. And it looked disgustingly crusty. Arg shuddered at the thought of even touching it. But if he could somehow knock it off, it might be enough. They could wet it and feed it to all the dinosaurs in the secret valley. It sounded like the perfect plan.

Arg saw a long branch lying in a tangle of ferns. He crawled over on all fours and carefully tugged it loose then crouched behind a cycad to wait.

The stegosaurus munched closer. And closer.

Arg's muscles tensed. Just a few more paces and then ...

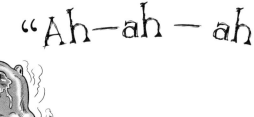

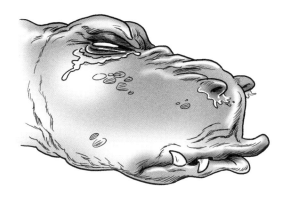

Skeet's sneeze shook the jungle. The stegosauruses jerked upright. There was no time to lose. Arg leapt out and swiped the branch at the stegosaurus's snotty snout. But he was too late. Its long neck swung away just out of reach.

screeeeeeeeeeeeecch!"

The entire herd started to gallop away from the ferocious predator screech. They didn't know it was just a sneeze. They thought a T-rex was coming to eat them.

T-rexes loved dining on stegosaur steaks.

Arg dropped the branch and gave chase.
He heard heavy footsteps lumbering behind.
He glanced over his shoulder ... and let out a huge
grunt of annoyance. Skeet was only trying to help.
But the sight of a huge T-rex striding closer sent the
frightened creatures into a panic.

Instead of crashing into the jungle, they circled back. Masses of moss and black showers of ooze splashed everywhere.

Arg screamed and leapt aside as a baby stego-saurus stampeded past. He landed heavily, right beside a big puddle of ooze. That was close!

He scrambled to his feet and dashed across the
clearing. The biggest stegosaur had found an escape
route back into the jungle. It gave a loud cry, calling
the rest of the herd towards it.

Arg's heart was nearly exploding in his chest.
But he couldn't stop now. He had to catch the
stegosaurus before it vanished in the jungle.

Arg dodged in and out of charging feet.

The biggest stegosaur barged into the jungle. The
barbed end of its tail slipped along the ground. Arg
ducked his head. With one last burst, he caught up.
He leapt onto its tail then sprinted up its back,
between the rows of spiky plates.

The stegosaurus swung its head to shake Arg
loose. Arg wrapped his arms around its neck and

held on tight. The stegosaurus herd crashed deeper into the jungle. Arg knew he had to act fast. With every second, he was being carried further from familiar trails. If the stegosaurs managed to lose Skeet, Arg might never find his way back.

But he wasn't going anywhere without some of that precious snot.

He braced his feet against a stegosaurus plate, then heaved himself up the stegosaur's neck. When he reached the head, he stretched one hand forward over the stegosaur's ear. His other hand stayed tightly curled around its neck. His fingers crept over the scaly skin until it felt the crusty snot clump.

He wedged his fingers under the edge. Then tugged with all his might. A snort of hot air and bubbly liquid blasted his fingertips. But the snot plug stayed firmly stuck.

Arg heaved himself higher. He hooked his legs around the bouncing, bounding stegosaur's neck and gripped the snot-plug firmly with both hands.

HEAVE! The plug wobbled.

HEAVE! The plug crackled and crumbled along its crusty edges.

It was moving! One more heave and ...

Without warning, the stegosaurus lurched ahead. Arg's hands shot forward like spears. They pierced the crust of snot and plunged into a gooey pool of rotting mucus. The smell hit Arg in the face like something long dead. Arg was soaked in snot up to his elbows.

The stegosaurus dug in its heels. Arg shot forward. As he jack-knifed over the stegosaur's head, his hands latched onto something inside the creature's snotty nostril. For a moment he swung from its chin like a beard.

Then the stegosaurus sneezed ...

Ahh . . . screeeech!

Arg rocketed to the ground in a shower of snot and mucus. He was drenched to the bone and felt like a big pile of pond scum, though he smelt much worse. But the worst part was that the stegosauruses were getting away! They were probably so scared now, they wouldn't come back for several moon cycles. Who knew how many dinosaurs would be dead by then? What a disaster. Arg felt like staying right where he was until the next thunderstorm.

Every time he moved, more snot trickled down his cloak. All he could do was bow his head in misery. And keep his mouth tightly shut.

He didn't look up, even when Skeet arrived.

"That was amazing!" cheered Skeet. "You were awesome! I would never have thought of gathering snot like that. You're so clever."

A thousand angry words sparked on Arg's tongue but he dared not open his mouth. So he remained silent, grunting angrily under his breath. He was very surprised when Skeet's tongue flicked along his cheek.

"Mmmmm," said Skeet, licking his lips, "that doesn't taste too bad at all."

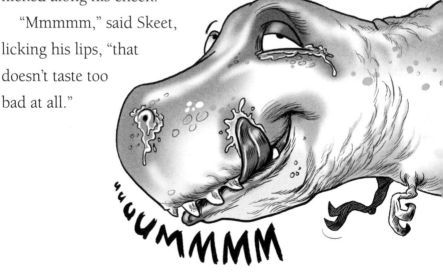

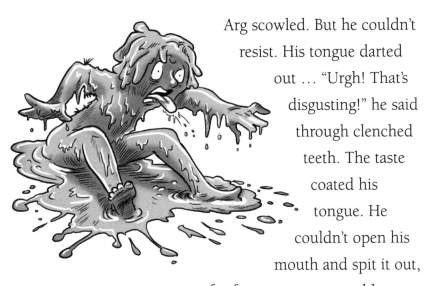

Arg scowled. But he couldn't resist. His tongue darted out ... "Urgh! That's disgusting!" he said through clenched teeth. The taste coated his tongue. He couldn't open his mouth and spit it out, for fear more snot would dribble inside. "You said it tasted good!"

Skeet laughed. "I didn't say it tasted *good*. I said it didn't taste bad ... for such a powerful medicine."

Arg struggled to his feet. The snot was already starting to dry. It was hard to move when everything was sticking together. He grabbed a big leaf and went to wipe off some of the snot. But Skeet stopped him.

"I've got a better idea," he said. "Why not kill two oviraptors with one chomp, as we T-rexes like to say?"

Arg felt stupid standing there like a statue while every dinosaur in the secret valley lined up to lick him. One of the raptors almost bit his head off. It was lucky Skeet was standing guard.

"Those raptors have only one thing on their minds – food," Skeet chuckled. Arg didn't think it was funny at all.

By the time the last dinosaur had licked him, Arg felt like he'd been in a sandstorm. Dinosaur tongues were very rough. His skin prickled painfully and he was covered in red spots. But at least every last trace of snot was gone.

Skeet gave Arg a ride back to the caves. Arg didn't say a word all the way. He slid off Skeet's back and trudged towards home.

"See you soon, Arg," called Skeet. "You did a great job! Thanks."

Arg gave a tired wave over his shoulder. But he didn't look back.

When Arg's mum saw him, she raced over, snatched him up and gave him a huge hug. Then she shook him.

Arg could tell she was confused. She didn't know if she was happy or angry. Her small brain couldn't manage to be two things at once.

"Me come back help Old Drik. Hng say Arg go cave bear," said Arg's mum. She stroked Arg like he was a prized mammoth fur. "Arg too smart go cave bear. But me worry. Cave bear bad."

Arg glanced at Hng. Her frown was even deeper than normal. Arg opened his mouth to explain, but it turned into a sneeze. "Ah-choo!"

"Arg sick. Arg go bed," said his mum. She carried him into the cave and dumped him on his bedrock. Krrk-Krrk jumped up and curled up against Arg's legs. "Me make powerful medicine. Make Arg better."

As Arg lay on his bedrock, waiting for his mum to return with one of her foul potions, a smile spread slowly across his face. He really *had* done a great job. The dinosaurs in the secret valley were safe from people flu now. Thanks to him and his friend Skeet.

And there was no way his mum's medicine could taste any worse than stegosaurus snot ... was there?

DINOSAUR RESCUE

KYLE MEWBURN & DONOVAN BIXLEY

VELOCITCHY-RAPTOR

CHAPTER ONE

Arg scooped up a big handful of diplodocus poo
and squelched it between his fingers. When it
was smooth and mushy, he dunked it in rotten
archaeopteryx egg yolk. Then he carefully mixed it
all together. The yolk turned the dark green poo into
the colour of a new cycad leaf.

It would be perfect ... if Arg was drawing a picture
of a cycad. But he wasn't. He was trying to draw a
cave boy covered in stegosaurus snot. It was part of
the story he was painting showing how he and Skeet
had saved the dinosaurs from people flu.

Arg gave an annoyed grunt and glanced over his
shoulder. The opposite wall was covered with Arg's
paintings. There were paintings of Arg's family,
paintings showing how his tribe lived, paintings of

his dad hunting and his mum making medicine. And there was a big painting of his sister Hng getting trampled by mastodons. (That was Arg's favourite, even though it was the only painting that never actually happened.) Along the top of the wall was a series of paintings telling the story of how Arg met Skeet.

Arg didn't know why he wanted to paint his stories. One day he just decided it was a good idea.

He was always having good ideas. It was probably
because he had a big brain.

Arg's mum always got worried when he had good
ideas. She said his Uncle Klug always had good
ideas too. Like one day he thought it
was a good idea to teach a sabre-
toothed tiger how to fetch and ...

Well, that's another story.

OW!

Arg scanned the rows of ingredients lined up on his painting stone. He had a whole collection of dinosaur poos. Every poo was a different shade of green. Except T-rex poo, which was a disgusting, smelly brown.

He had lots of half eggshells full of rotten yolk, blood, fungus and different kinds of moss. And little piles of brightly-coloured dirt. Maybe if he mixed allosaurus poo with pond scum and ...

Arg's nose started twitching.

"Not again," he huffed as his cave filled with smoke.

By the time Arg reached the main cave, his eyes were streaming with tears. His family were sitting in a haze of thick smoke. Their eyes were as red as embers. But they didn't mind. Arg's mum was busy chewing a big scab off her knee. His sister, Hng, was dangling giant slugs above the coals. She smiled as they squirmed and frothed. Arg's dad was dragging a soggy log over to the fire.

Arg hurried over and grabbed his dad's arm.

"Why don't you use the dry logs?" asked Arg.

"Uhn?" his dad grunted.

"You know. The dry logs? Just there," said Arg. He pointed at the massive pile of dry wood in the corner.

His dad grinned. Finally he understood.

But as soon as Arg let go, his dad tossed the sodden log onto the smouldering fire. A cloud of stinky black smoke filled Arg's lungs and painted his face with soot.

Coughing and spluttering, Arg rushed to the cave entrance. Sometimes it was hard being the only one with a big brain.

Arg's mum likes smoking (she thinks it makes her look cool)

Arg's dad listens to Rock (he's an old-school head banger)

How to talk to Stone Age people

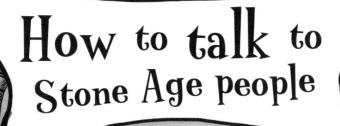

Talking to Stone Age people is very hard because they don't have many words.
It is also very boring because all they want to talk about is food. The only people more boring to talk to than Stone Age people are little sisters. All they want to talk about is ponies and fairies.

If Stone Age people want to explain something complicated, they usually use sign language. It can be very dangerous, because different tribes use different signs. In most tribes, holding your nose means something stinks. But in Grogllgrox tribes, it means "Can I cut off your head and scoop out your brain?" So you should never agree. Actually, you shouldn't be trying to talk to a Grogllgrox in the first place. They are very blood-thirsty. If you see a Grogllgrox, the best thing to do is run. Fast. If a Grogllgrox invites you to dinner, you should always say no. Because you are the dinner!

If Stone Age people want to tell a long story, they paint pictures on the wall. Stone Age mums don't mind, because their walls don't have wallpaper. And housework hasn't been invented yet.

Stone Age people are terrible at Maths, too. Even if they count on their fingers, they never get to eleven.
They go 1 ... 2 ... 3 ... LOTS.
Arg once made a counting-stuff-thing with sticks and seeds. Each little seed was worth one thing. Bigger seeds were ten things. And really big seeds were a hundred things.

312

He called his invention an Argacus. It worked really well until it got wet. Then all the seeds started sprouting ... and his mum ate it.

CHAPTER TWO

Outside, rain poured down on the village like a waterfall. A fierce storm had been battering the valley for seven suns. Jagged forks of flame lit up the sky and the world shook as if a giant brontosaurus was farting in the sky.

The village was deserted. Everyone was too afraid to go outside. They all thought the world was going to end ... again.

Arg used to think the world was going to end, too. Because that's what everyone said. But each time there was another storm, and the world *didn't* end, he got less scared. Now he knew storms didn't mean anything. They just happened sometimes.

He wasn't afraid anymore ... well, maybe just a little bit.

S-C-R-E-E-E-E-E-E-E-E-C-H!!!!

A fierce cry echoed through the valley, loud enough to drown out the thunder. It sounded a bit like his T-rex friend, Skeet. Maybe he needed Arg's help to rescue some dinosaurs.

Arg looked one way then the other.

A huge shape swooped low over the treetops. Then it plunged into the canopy. Arg's mouth gaped open. It wasn't Skeet, it was a Quetzalcoatlus! Arg had never seen one up close before. They were very rare. And very, very fierce.

"Come on, Krrk-krrk!" said Arg. "Let's go and see what it's doing."

At the cave entrance there were four sticks and a dried devil frog. Arg quickly shoved a stick into each of the frog's flippers, then stretched it as wide as it could go.

As he stepped out of the cave, he lifted the frog over his head. The rain pounded on the devil frog like a drum. But Arg stayed completely dry ... well, *almost* completely. Arg called his invention an underella.

He got ten steps before he realised Krrk-krrk wasn't at his feet. Krrk-krrk went everywhere with Arg. But not this time.

"It's not raining *that* hard," Arg lied. The bottom of his coat was already soaked and his legs were splattered with mud. Krrk-krrk stayed yapping at the cave entrance. "Suit yourself," said Arg.

Without his underella, Arg would have been drenched in seconds. But it slowed him down a lot, too. Hopefully the Quetzalcoatlus didn't fly away before Arg got to see it close up ...

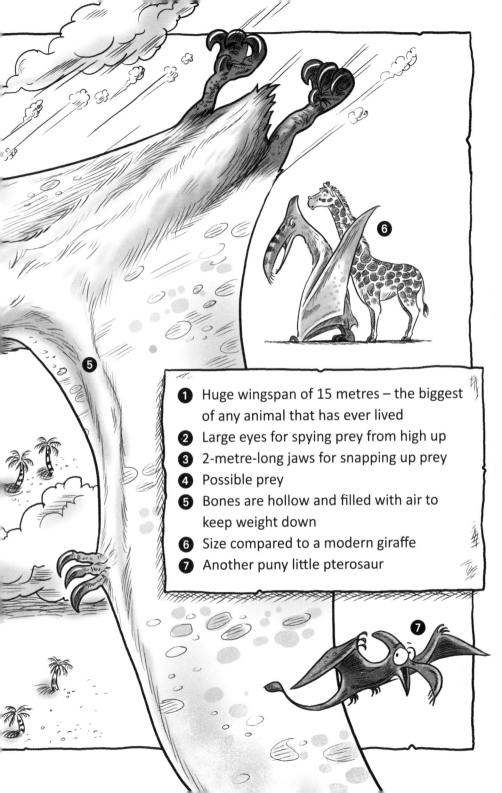

1. Huge wingspan of 15 metres – the biggest of any animal that has ever lived
2. Large eyes for spying prey from high up
3. 2-metre-long jaws for snapping up prey
4. Possible prey
5. Bones are hollow and filled with air to keep weight down
6. Size compared to a modern giraffe
7. Another puny little pterosaur

Arg's underella started jerking and twisting wildly in his hands. It felt as if something was trying to snatch it from his grasp. Arg got ready to fight off the sneaky underella snatcher.

But there wasn't any snatcher. It was his underella! It was *alive*!

The devil frog squirmed and twisted, trying to get its flippers free. It kept blinking its eyes like it had

just woken up. And it wasn't flat any more. It was big and round ... and getting bigger every second.

Its mouth opened wide, revealing rows of tiny, razor-sharp teeth. Then a long, barbed tongue flicked out and wrapped around Arg's arm.

"Let go, you stupid frog!" yelled Arg.

Suddenly, the leaves started trembling. A rush of air swept along the path.

The hair on the back of Arg's neck stood up. So did the thick stripe of hair down his spine. Arg spun around. He *was* going to see a Quetzalcoatlus close up after all. A lot, LOT closer than he wanted.

The Quetzalcoatlus shot along the path, heading straight towards him. It was as twice as big as a pterodactyl, and it was moving faster than a meteor!

There was no time to duck.

Whoooooooooooooooshh

The Quetzalcoatlus snatched the devil frog in its
beak, then shot skywards. Arg squealed as his feet
left the ground. He twisted and tugged the frog's
tongue, trying to break free. But it was hooked
around the sleeve of his coat.

In two heartbeats they were above the jungle.
Higher and higher the Quetzalcoatlus soared,

KRRAQOM

almost into the clouds. The thunder was deafening. Lightning bolts scorched past, close enough to singe Arg's hair. The rain was sharp as spearheads. Arg shut his eyes and held on tight.

When the Quetzalcoatlus finally started to dive, Arg glanced down. Far below, he saw clouds of steam rising from the bubbling geysers of Slimepot Swamp. At least they were still in his valley.

With a fearsome flap of its massive wings, the
Quetzalcoatlus landed on a pile of branches and
dinosaur bones that was perched on a narrow ledge.
It flicked its head, sending the frog and Arg tumbling
into the centre of the pile.

The frog blinked then hopped one way. Arg scuttled the other way. He hoped Quetzalcoatluses thought frogs tasted better than cave boys. But he wasn't taking any chances. He tugged a branch loose from the pile. If the Quetzalcoatlus tried to eat him, it was going to get a whack on the beak.

The Quetzalcoatlus didn't try to eat Arg. Or the devil frog. It gave an ear-piercing S-C-R-E-E-C-H, then flew away.

Arg scratched his head. Quetzalcoatluses were fierce predators. They could kill an allosaur with one flash of their razor-sharp claws. Yet Arg and the frog were both still alive. It didn't make sense.

Unless ...

Arg slowly looked around. The ground was thick with feathers, Quetzalcoatlus poo and animal skulls. It *did* make sense after all. This wasn't just any old pile of branches and bones. It was a nest!

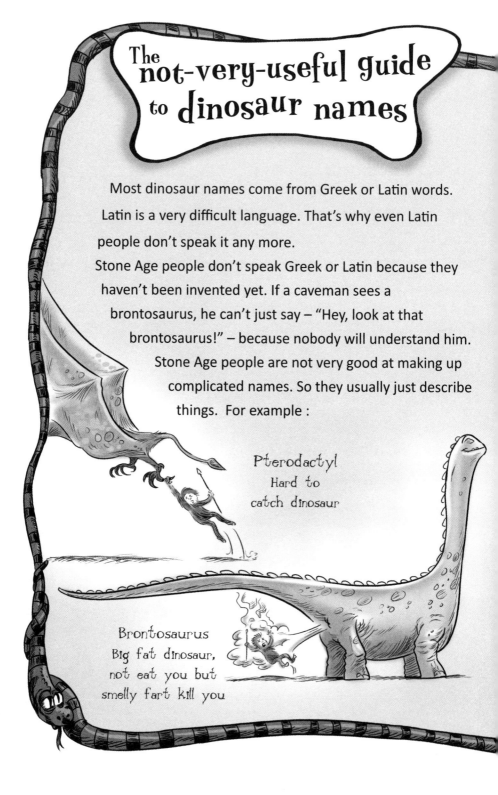

The not-very-useful guide to dinosaur names

Most dinosaur names come from Greek or Latin words. Latin is a very difficult language. That's why even Latin people don't speak it any more.

Stone Age people don't speak Greek or Latin because they haven't been invented yet. If a caveman sees a brontosaurus, he can't just say – "Hey, look at that brontosaurus!" – because nobody will understand him. Stone Age people are not very good at making up complicated names. So they usually just describe things. For example :

Pterodactyl
Hard to
catch dinosaur

Brontosaurus
Big fat dinosaur,
not eat you but
smelly fart kill you

Tyrannosaurus rex
Scary dinosaur
make you run away
screaming like girl

EEEK

Ankylosaurus
Hard to kill dinosaur

Triceratops
Dumb dinosaur with
sharp hurty bits

Allosaurus
Big yummy dinosaur

Oviraptor
Little yummy dinosaur

If a Stone Age person tried to say Quetzalcoatlus, their brain would explode and their tongue would fall off.

CHAPTER THREE

Arg circled the nest, searching frantically for an exit.
The walls were too steep to climb. And the pelting
rain had turned the poo into a slippery mess.

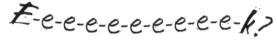

E-e-e-e-e-e-e-e-e-e-k?

Arg froze. There was something moving deep inside the nest wall. Arg tightened his grip round his club and peered closer.

E-e-e-e-e-e-e-e-e-k?

Arg leapt back as a brightly coloured head popped out. The velociraptor was nearly as big as Arg. But he could tell by its feathers it was a baby. It wasn't dangerous. It was just scared. Like Arg.

Velociraptor

1. Large brain – the 2nd largest of any dinosaur (relative to size)
2. Body covered in feathers (which may cause itching)
3. Winglike arms – velociraptors are related to the flying dinosaur archeopteryx and modern birds
4. Huge, sickle-like claw can rotate 300 degrees. Claws are used for slashing and also climbing trees to glide down from
5. Colourful display feathers – unfortunately they look very dull in black and white

4
An interesting point

The velociraptor rubbed its feathery cheeks against Arg's chest and made strange purring noises.

"Don't worry," Arg laughed. "I'll get us ou—ou—*achoo!*"

Arg's nose filled with snot and his skin started to tingle. The tingle quickly turned into a painful itchy burny feeling. It felt like he was being attacked by fire ants. Except they must be *invisible* fire ants because he couldn't see them.

Arg scooped up some Quetzalcoatlus poo and rubbed it over his skin. That was the only cure for fire ants. (At least that's what his mum said.) But it just made it worse.

A blast of hot, foul-smelling air filled the nest. Arg looked up. His jaw dropped. He forgot all about the invisible fire ants. He had a much, MUCH bigger problem to worry about now ...

Like the huge Quetzalcoatlus chick perched on the edge of the nest above.

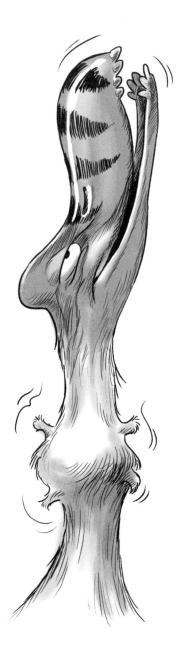

The chick was nearly full grown. Its wings spanned the nest. Its claws were as big as Arg. Its beady eyes bounced from the devil frog to Arg, then back to the devil frog. It looked hungry.

The devil frog started hopping frantically against the wall. But there was no escape. A pointy beak speared down and grabbed the frog's leg.

With one flick, the frog was tossed into the air. It did a double somersault, then disappeared down the chick's gaping beak.

Arg watched the lump squeeze down the chick's throat. If he didn't find a way out, he was next on the menu.

He spun round. Where had the velociraptor gone?
From deep inside the nest wall, he heard a faint
E-e-e-e-e-k? Maybe there *was* a way out! Arg
squeezed between two poo-splattered branches,
clambered over a slippery bone and pushed between
a curtain of thorny vines ...

Suddenly he was standing outside the nest, beside
the velociraptor.

He was free ... sort of.

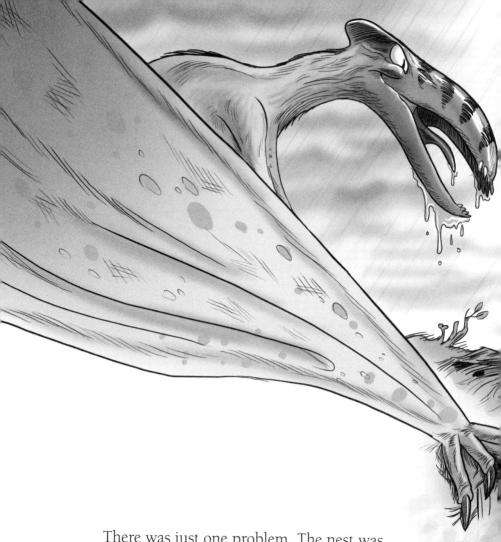

There was just one problem. The nest was perched on the edge of a vertical cliff. There were no paths, no rocky outcrops to hold on to. And it was a very long way down. If only velociraptors could fly.

That's it! thought Arg.

228

He scrambled back into the nest, snatched up two giant Quetzalcoatlus feathers and dragged them outside. They were taller than Arg, but light as ... well, feathers.

S-C-R-E-E-E-E-E-E-E-E-C-H!

The Quetzalcoatlus chick scuttled across its nest until it was directly above Arg. It wasn't going to let its dinner escape that easily. It lunged downwards.

There was no time to think. Arg gripped a feather tightly in each hand, then jumped. It was better to splatter on the ground than to get gobbled by a Quetzalcoatlus.

The wind caught Arg's feathers and lifted him.

He was flying! He was FLYING! He was ...

E-e-e-e-e-k?

The velociraptor leapt off the cliff and landed
on Arg's back. Arg flapped his arms furiously. But he
wasn't flying any more ... he was falling!

Arg scrunched his eyes closed and held his breath. He hoped it was over quickly. Together, he and the velociraptor were going to make a big mess. Some scavenger would be very happy – unless the ground was so soft they sank straight into the mud and vanished. Then, many, many, MANY moons from now (when everyone had big brains like Arg), someone would find his body and realise he was the first person

AMARGASAUR

in the world to have a big brain. He'd be famous!

Unless they thought the velociraptor's bones were his bones. Then they'd think he was a clever dinosaur, like Skeet. They might stick his head and arms on the velociraptor's body. They'd call it an Argosaurus and put him in a museum. That would be funny ... if he knew what a museum was.

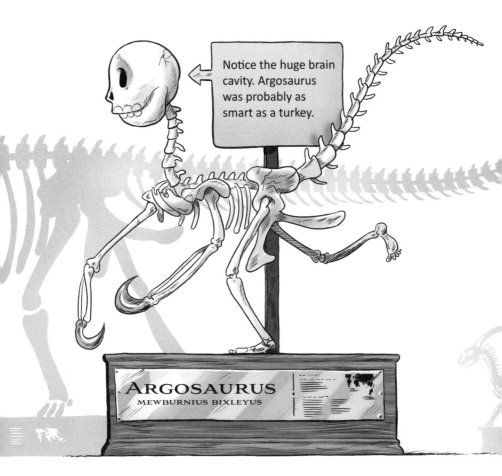

But what if he *didn't* get splattered? What if
he just broke all his bones? Then he'd have to lie
there until a sabre-toothed tiger came along and
ripped him apart. Or a Grogllgrox found him and
scooped out his brains. He might even dry Arg's skin
and put it on the floor of his cave. Or maybe ...

Arg sighed. That was the problem with having a
big brain. He couldn't stop thinking. Sometimes he
wished he could turn his brain off. Like right now.

E-e-e-e-e-k?

The velociraptor didn't sound scared. He sounded
excited. His claws were hooked tightly on Arg's coat.
Maybe he was too stupid to be scared. Or maybe ...

Arg opened one eye just a crack. He expected to
see the ground rushing towards him like a fist. But it
was flowing underneath him like a river. The flaps of
skin under the velociraptor's arms were puffed up
with wind. Its tail was spread wide like a fan.

They weren't falling.

They were gliding!

Arg held his arms out like wings. In a few seconds, they'd be back on the ground, not far from where the Quetzalcoatlus snatched Arg.

"I'm saved!" he yelled. "I'm ... uh-oh ..."

The ground rushed up to meet them. The velociraptor started flapping his arms wildly, but it was too late. They hit the forest floor in a geyser of mud and leaves, then started sliding down the hill. Faster and faster.

CHAPTER FOUR

Arg gurgled and gasped for breath as his face ploughed a deep furrow through the ground. The velociraptor rode on his back, squealing with delight.

Together they slid and slurped then finally squelched to a halt.

Arg peeled himself out of the mud and spat out a mouthful of leaves. He was covered in mud from head to toe. He looked like one of the blobby clay figures Old Drik made. Her cave was full of them. She said they scared away evil spirits. But Arg's mum said they just scared away husbands. Like once, when Old Drik was young, she ...

But that's another story.

The velociraptor waddled closer. It tried to rub its feathery cheeks against Arg's chest again but Arg pushed it away.

"Thanks for saving me," said Arg. "But I have to go ah–ah–ahh … CHOO!"

E-e-e-e-e-k? The velociraptor didn't budge.

"Look," said Arg. "If you come home with me someone will eat you. I'm not allowed pets. My mum and dad only let me keep Krrk-Krrk because he's too small to eat. Sometimes my sister Hng tries to eat him anyway."

The velociraptor stepped closer and shook his feathers.

"Ahh … CHOOO!" went Arg again.

Those feathers! thought Arg. *That's what's making me sneeze.*

Arg's previous pets

Arg's pet
archeopteryx
(after Hng found it)

Arg's pet
cave bear
(after it got too big
one cold winter)

Arg's pet rocks — finally, a safe pet

Rock group   Rock star   Rock bottom

Actually, they weren't just making Arg sneeze. His eyes felt as if someone had rubbed sand in them. His nose was stuffed solid. And every inch of skin was breaking out in itchy, flaming sores. If he didn't get far away from the velociraptor soon ...

Arg started sprinting as fast as he could.

The velociraptor caught him in a flash. But the path wasn't wide enough for both of them. The velociraptor jostled and bumped alongside, flapping its feathered arms.

"Go away, you stupid velocira—ahhh ... CHOO!"

AHHHHHHHH

Arg's sneeze threw him off balance. He dug in his heels, but they kept sliding on the mud. The path veered left. Arg kept going straight ahead. He crashed through a curtain of cycad fronds then splashed, face first, into a pool of stagnant water.

The velociraptor bent down and nudged Arg with its head.

E-e-e-e-e-e-k?

Arg spat out a mouthful of algae and tugged a huge leech out of his nose.

Stupid velociraptor, thought Arg. *This time I'm going to ...*

Arg opened his mouth to yell, but it turned into a sigh. The velociraptor wasn't stupid. It was scared. It didn't want to be left alone in the dark jungle. Arg could understand that. It was just a baby. It would get eaten in no time.

If he took the velociraptor to the secret valley, Skeet could look after it until it grew up.

There was just one problem. It was almost dark. Somehow, he'd have to hide the velociraptor in his cave overnight. If anyone found it, they were both in huge trouble.

Hiding food from your tribe was the worst thing a Neanderthal could do. The velociraptor would get eaten and Arg would be banished forever. Arg's sister would do anything to make sure that happened.

The storm was getting fiercer. The whole valley shook like an avalanche. Every few heartbeats, a blinding fork of flame spat from the clouds.

Trees split in half and crashed to the ground. Arg had
to dodge and weave around burning branches ...

and dead giant sloths, smouldering on the path.
Maybe the world *was* going to end this time.

The velociraptor didn't leave Arg's side. It didn't make a sound, either.

Arg paused on the edge of the clearing. The village was deserted. He'd probably make it to his family's cave without anyone seeing him. But how was he supposed to get a velociraptor past his mum and dad? They might not be very clever, but they could smell food from ten spear-throws away. And if Hng found out ...

He didn't even want to think about that.

Arg took a deep breath. "Come on," he whispered. The velociraptor yawned. It was getting very sleepy.

As they crept towards the cave, Arg picked up a spear from beside the flint pile. If anyone saw him, he'd pretend he was trying to catch the velociraptor. Everyone would believe him. Nobody could imagine he was actually trying to sneak a velociraptor into his cave.

He would hate to watch his dad kill the velociraptor. But he'd hate it even more if he got banished.
Besides, velociraptors were very tasty.

They reached the cave entrance unseen.

Now what? wondered Arg.

The velociraptor yawned again. It stretched its arms and unfolded its tail. Its feathers shimmered blue and red. Its skin glimmered gold. A velociraptor skin would make a very nice coat ...

That was it!

Arg grinned.

More than 3 astounding facts about Stone Age food

1. Food is very important to Stone Age tribes. If Stone Age people don't eat food, they will die. They need water, too. But water is NOT food ... unless it is swamp water. Then it might contain all sorts of things like mosquito larvae, tadpoles and algae. Which is kind of food.

Pure water

2. Stone Age people will eat almost anything. They don't care if it's raw or cooked, alive or dead, or crawling with maggots. Sometimes they eat poisonous things by mistake. If they don't die, they will know it's poisonous next time ... unless they forget. If they can't remember if something is poisonous or not, they feed it to an old person first. Most Stone Age people don't live very long.

3. Stone Age people share all their food. But they don't share equally. The men eat first. They eat as much as they can. Then the women and children eat the left-

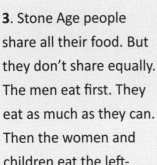

After some 'tasting'

overs. The women don't mind, because while they are cooking they do a lot of 'tasting'. By the time the meal's ready, they are usually not very hungry. Once the women and children have eaten, the old people get to gnaw on the bones. Sometimes they accidentally gnaw on each other's bones.

Lots. Stone Age people don't have refrigerators. Or freezers. So they have to eat all their food right away. If there is a nearby glacier, they can store extra food in it for a few days. It is not a good idea to store food inside a glacier for too long. Unlike most freezers, glaciers are always moving. If food is left in a glacier too long, it can be very difficult to retrieve.

CHAPTER FIVE

"Hi, Mum! Hi, Dad!" Arg called as he cut across the main cave, carrying the snoring velociraptor on his back. The velociraptor's arms were clasped around Arg's neck, its long tail dragged on the floor. Arg's whole body burned with itchy sores. It felt like he'd been dipped in lava. He hoped his mum didn't notice.

His mum and dad peered at him through the smoke. His sister ignored him as usual. She was too busy pulling legs off a giant centipede.

"What Arg get?" asked his mum suspiciously. She sniffed the air.

"It's my new velociraptor cloak," said Arg. He spun around to show them the velociraptor's bright, feathered tail. "Do you like it?"

His mum and dad looked at each other. Then shrugged. They hardly ever understood what Arg was doing.

Arg breathed a sigh of relief. He was going to make it.

Krrk-Krrk came rushing out to meet Arg. He jumped up, wagging his tail. Then he saw the velociraptor.

"Shhhh," hissed Arg, as Krrk-Krrk started yapping wildly.

Krrk-Krrk backed away, growling. His feet kicked up tiny clouds of dust.

"Go away!" said Arg.

The velociraptor lifted its head and fluffed up its cheek feathers.

"Ahhh ..."

Arg raced towards his cave. If he sneezed, his mum would want to check him right away. She thought sneezes were caused by evil spirits. There was no way she wouldn't see the velociraptor. Then he would be doomed.

"Ahhhhh ..."

Arg glanced across at his parents. They weren't paying any attention. He was going to make it. He was ...

Through the smoke he saw his sister Hng watching him. As he ducked into his cave, she gave him an evil smile.

"Ahhhh-CHOOOOO! Ahhhh-CHOOOOO!"

Arg couldn't stop sneezing. His sneezes echoed through the cave. There was no time to lose. He jumped on his bed-rock and held the velociraptor tightly to his chest. Then he grabbed his cave-bear blanket and pulled it up to his neck.

Ahhhh—CHOOOOOO!

The velociraptor's tail was sticking out the end but there was no time to cover it.

His mum padded towards him. She was carrying her medicine bag.

Arg gulped with fear. If he had a choice between

259

being banished and being cured by his mum, he
knew which one he'd choose. But if he tried to run
now, the velociraptor would get killed.

His mum felt his forehead. She tugged out his
tongue and scrubbed it roughly with her finger.

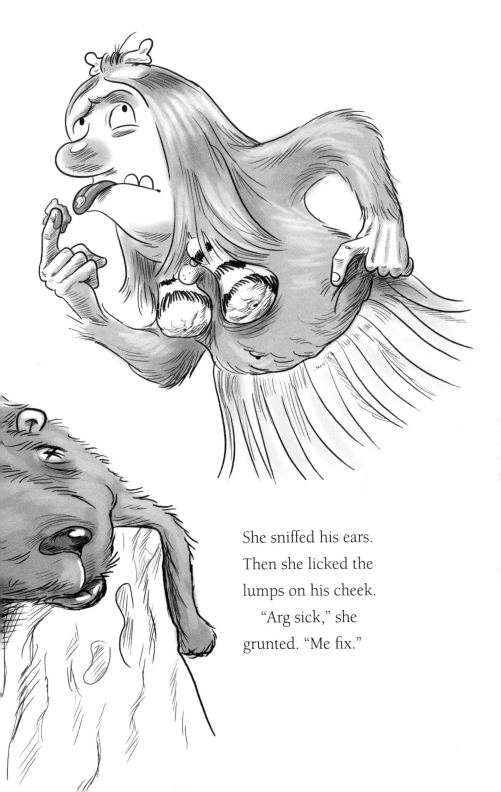

She sniffed his ears.
Then she licked the
lumps on his cheek.
"Arg sick," she
grunted. "Me fix."

She fished a large snail shell from her bag and dipped her finger inside. When she pulled her finger out, it was coated in stinky black goo. It smelt exactly like the stuff his mum scraped from under Old Drik's toenails every moon. She rubbed it on her hands, then started smearing it over Arg's face.

Arg's stomach lurched. It *was* the stuff his mum scraped from under Old Drik's toenails. He gritted his teeth. The smell was disgusting.

But ... wait a second ... his sores were already starting to feel better ... in fact, he was feeling pretty good altogether ... if the room just stopped spinning for a second, he'd ...

Arg fell into a deep, dreamless sleep.

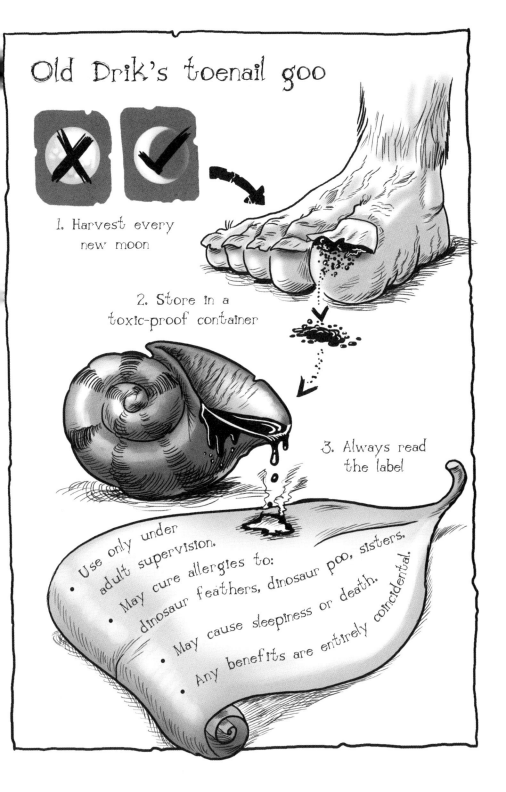

In the middle of the night, Arg's instincts woke him up. He heard footsteps creeping closer. As his eyes opened sleepily, a shape leapt out of the shadows.

"La-la-la-la-la-la-la-la-la-la-la!"

Arg's blood froze. He knew that sound. It was Hng's war-cry.

Arg threw himself sideways. As he tumbled to the floor, a loud **THUNK!** echoed through his cave. Arg knew that sound, too. It was the sound of a spear piercing flesh.

"No!" yelled Arg.

"Arg go! Arg go!" grunted Hng. Her eyes gleamed evilly in the light of the dying embers.

Arg's parents stumbled into the cave, rubbing
their eyes. Arg's dad was carrying a flaming torch.
The cave danced with shadows.

"Arg hide food," said Hng. "Arg go! Arg go!
Arg ... uhn?"

She turned to gloat over her prey. But there was
no sign of a velociraptor. Just a spear stuck in the
head of Arg's cave-bear blanket.

Arg's mum and dad looked at Hng. Then looked at each other. With a weary shrug, they turned away. They loved both their children equally. But sometimes they wished they weren't both so weird. Why couldn't they have normal children like Shlok and Gurg?

* R.I.P.
Ripped In Pieces

Hng refused to admit defeat. She pulled her spear from the cave bear's head and attacked the blanket as if it were still alive. She was sure the velociraptor was hiding under there somewhere.

Arg scratched his head. He was glad that the

velociraptor hadn't been in his bed when Hng
attacked … but where was it?

As his parents ducked through the cave entrance,
their torch caught a flash of blue and red. The
velociraptor was curled up on the ledge above.

"Nice try, Hng," said Arg.

At the first hint of dawn, Arg gently lifted the
velociraptor from its cosy perch. The storm had
finally passed and the morning was eerily quiet.
Arg carried the sleeping velociraptor all the way
to the secret valley.

Arg's flaming sores had filled with pus overnight.
He looked like an ankylosaurus with blisters. But at
least his skin wasn't burning any more. Maybe his
mum knew about medicine after all. Or maybe he
was just getting used to the velociraptor's feathers.

Arg found Skeet playing with two
young stygimolochs beside the
secret valley's crystal lake.

Skeet T-Wreck-asaurus

1. Massive jaws for talking your ear off
2. Huge teeth – up to 23cm long
3. Pathetic little arms – useless for just about everything
4. Powerful legs – can run at 25km per hour
5. Absolutely ginormous brain. Note that it is 10 times the size of a normal dinosaur brain!
6. Long tail – counterbalances the weight of that HUGE brain

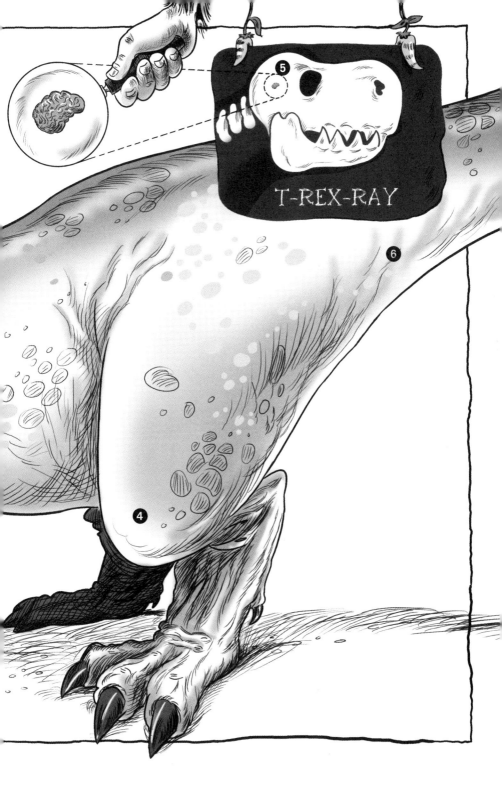

T-REX-RAY

"What happened to you?" asked Skeet. "You look terrible."

"It's a long story," said Arg. "I'll paint it for you one day. Is it all right if this velociraptor stays here?"

"Of course," said Skeet. "I'm sure the other velociraptors will take very good care of it. Where did you find it?"

"In a Quetzalcoatlus nest," said Arg. "Its chick nearly ate us both."

"A Quetzalcoatlus nest!" said Skeet. "That must have been scary. Quetzalcoatluses even make *me* nervous."

"It wasn't *that* scary," Arg lied.

"Do you want to come and meet the velociraptor's new family?" asked Skeet.

Arg did, really. But it was probably better if the velociraptor met its new family alone. Besides, his sores were starting to get itchy again.

"Maybe next time," said Arg, scratching his cheek. Thick green pus exploded onto his finger.

YUK!

Arg grinned. It was just the colour he'd been looking for! Finally, he could finish painting the story about how they'd saved the dinosaurs from people flu.

He had a new story to paint now, too. He couldn't wait to start.

At the entrance to the exit tunnel, Arg stopped to watch a flock of archaeopteryxes wheeling in the sky. The cliff was dotted with nests. The rocks were stained with archaeopteryx poo. The archaeopteryxes must have been eating ungberries, because their poo was bright blue.

That poo would be perfect for painting velociraptor feathers, thought Arg.

All he had to do was climb up and get some. Surely the archaeopteryxes wouldn't mind …

DINOSAUR RESCUE

KYLE MEWBURN & DONOVAN BIXLEY

DIPLO-DIZZYDOCUS

How to tell if Hng is being evil

1. YES
she is awake

2. NO
she is asleep
(although possibly
still having evil
dreams)

CHAPTER ONE

When Arg saw his sister, Hng, creeping through the village, he knew right away she was up to no good. Not because she was carrying an enormous pinecone. Or because she kept glancing around to make sure nobody was watching. (Even though that was a bit suspicious.) The main reason was because Hng was smiling. Hng only smiled when she was being evil.

Arg couldn't imagine what Hng was planning. He suspected it was some kind of mean prank. Arg liked playing pranks, too. But his pranks were never nasty. Not on purpose, anyway. Sometimes they just didn't go exactly according to plan. Like one time he thought it would be funny if he covered a lava pit with cycad fronds and ...

But that's another story.

Arg's Family Tree

Mum   Dad

 Arg

Hng

Arg's descendants – Millions of years later – Hng's descendants

 LeonArgo
da Vinci

 Hngis
Khan

 Attilla
the Hng

Wolfgang
Argadeus
Mozart

Albert
Argstein

K-Hng Kong
(a throwback
from the ape side
of the family)

Arg usually tried to stay as far away from Hng as possible. Hng was very dangerous. Especially to Arg. She didn't like it that Arg had a bigger brain than her. But he couldn't stay away this time. All the hunters were away hunting. All the gatherers were out gathering. Only old people and children were left behind. There was nobody to stop Hng's prank from hurting someone. Except Arg.

"Come on, Shlok," whispered Arg. "We better keep an eye on Hng."

Shlok leapt up. He was always ready for action. He looked wildly around.

He didn't know how to
keep an eye on
someone. So he
picked up a sharp
stone and hurled it at
Hng. Lucky for Arg, Shlok was
a terrible shot. The stone went whizzing
past Hng's ear and smashed into a tree on the
other side of the clearing.

"I meant follow her," said Arg, rolling his
eyes. Shlok was Arg's best friend. But sometimes he
wasn't very smart. Actually, he was *never* very smart.

Hng crept around the flint pile, then darted across
to where the old men were sleeping under a big tree.
Arg and Shlok kept a safe distance behind, making
sure they stayed downwind.

The old men were supposed to be cracking bungel nuts. But it was hard work when you didn't have any teeth. Their chins were stained red with bungel juice. They looked like they'd all been knocked out in a fight.

Old Kril was sitting cross-legged on top of the lookout rock. He was supposed to be guarding the village in case they got attacked. His eyes were open and he was holding his spear. But Arg could hear him snoring.

The sound of splashing and
yelling drifted across the clearing.
All the other children were playing
in the hot mud pools. The old women
were sitting around the fire pit, fishing
charred bones from the ashes and sucking
out the marrow. Except for Old Drik.
She was busy arguing with a tree.

Hng tiptoed from one sleeping man to the
next. Each time, she shook something out of the
pinecone and carefully stuck it up a sleeping man's
nose. They looked like pine seeds. But why would
Hng put pine seeds in their noses?

Hng shook the pinecone again. One of the seeds
sprouted wings and buzzed away. It flew across the
clearing and landed on Shlok's chin.

It wasn't a pine seed. It was a
stink bug. A geyser stink bug.
They were the stinkiest
stink bugs by far.

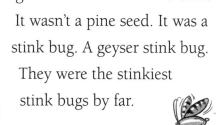

The Geyser Stink Bug

1. Do you really need me to tell you what this is?
2. Smell-sensitive hairs on legs and antennae help detect the stinkiest poo
3. Semi-transparent body (you can see poo fermenting in stomach acids, producing revolting gases that swell body to twice its size – eventually gases explode from the you-know-what)
4. Tiny eyes – stink bug has little use for vision
5. Long tongue for licking up poo
6. Actual size

Shlok's hand swept towards his chin.

"Don't do that!" hissed Arg. But he was too late.

Splat!

The stink bug exploded, spraying putrid yellow goo everywhere. Shlok jolted upright ... well, almost upright. His eyes were spinning and his hair was standing up all over his body.

He looked like he'd been struck by lightning.
Luckily, Arg couldn't smell anything.

His nose had been stuffed with snot for days.
Most of the time he could hardly breathe.

It took a few seconds for the smell to make it from
Shlok's nose to his brain. Then ...

"Ye-e-e-e-a-a-a-argh!"

Shlok spun around in screaming circles, then
raced off into the jungle.

Arg threw himself behind the flint pile. If Hng saw him ... Arg didn't even want to think about that. When he finally poked his head out, there was no sign of Hng. And the old men were still dozing peacefully. That was strange.

A rustle of leaves made Arg look up. Hng was clambering up the tree like a primate. Up and up she climbed until the branches got so thin, they could hardly support her weight. They started to sway and creak. If she climbed much higher, a branch was sure

to snap, sending her crashing down. Hng couldn't be that dumb … could she?

Hng stopped climbing and started inching her way along a long, bendy branch. When she was directly over the sleeping old men, she started shaking the tree. Harder and harder. Clouds of pollen and dust rained down.

Arg's eyes widened in surprise. Hng wasn't dumb at all. In fact, she was dangerously clever.

The pollen and dust covered the old men in a yellow blanket. It made their fur itch and their noses twitch. Sleepy hands flopped on twitchy faces. Noses wriggled. Fingers scratched and picked. But their noses kept getting itchier with each breath.

With annoyed grunts, they squeezed their noses tightly shut.

"Ye-e-e-e-a-a-argh!" The old men screamed as the stink bugs exploded in their noses. They leapt to their feet and ran in wild circles, bouncing and crashing into each other. They were so shocked, they forgot they were old. They kept hitting their noses with their fists. They didn't understand what was happening. They just wanted the smell to stop.

High up in the tree, Hng watched with an evil grin.

If Arg didn't act fast, someone would get hurt.

He looked around frantically. When he saw Skeet, his T-rex friend, standing on the edge of the jungle, he didn't know what to do.

Skeet was waving his tiny arms to attract Arg's attention. Some dinosaurs must be in terrible danger for Skeet to risk coming so close to Arg's village. But Arg couldn't just leave the old men alone, could he?

The village erupted with cries as the old women rushed to help. Arg breathed a sigh of relief. The old men would be all right now. He hurried to join Skeet. They had some dinosaurs to rescue.

299

Skeet T-Wreck-asaurus

1. Massive jaws for talking your ear off
2. Huge teeth – up to 23cm long
3. Pathetic little arms – useless for just about everything
4. Powerful legs – can run at 25km per hour
5. Absolutely ginormous brain. Note that it is 10 times the size of a normal dinosaur brain!
6. Long tail – counterbalances the weight of that HUGE brain

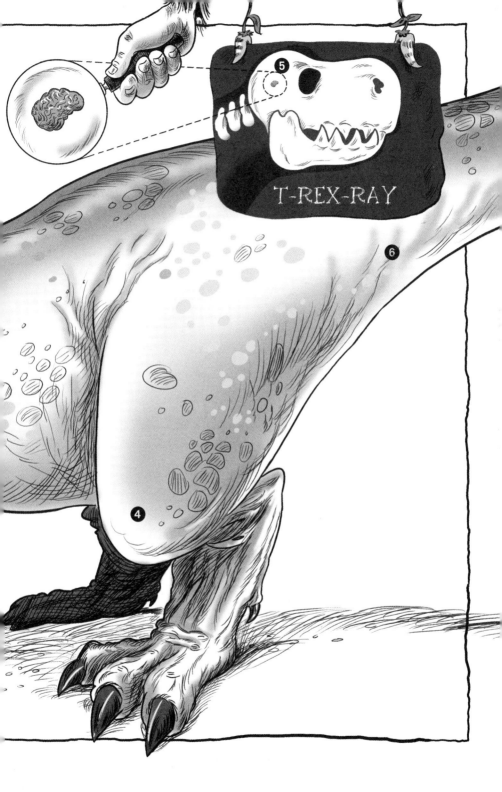

Fascinating facts about Stone Age School

Phoenecian

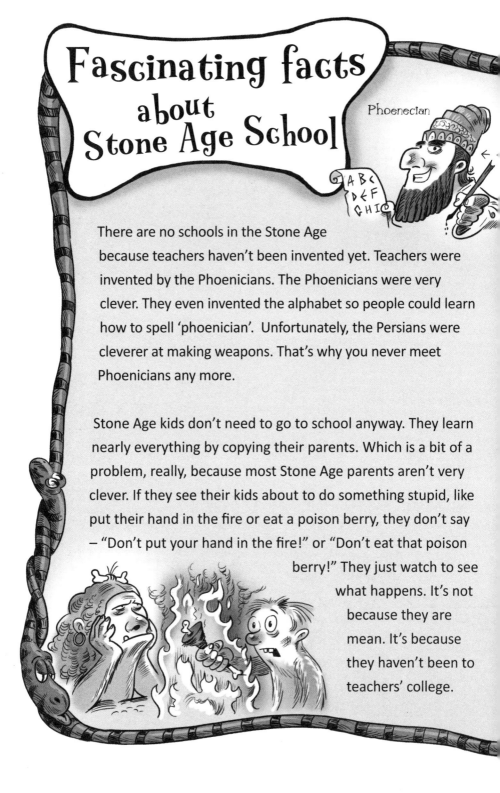

There are no schools in the Stone Age because teachers haven't been invented yet. Teachers were invented by the Phoenicians. The Phoenicians were very clever. They even invented the alphabet so people could learn how to spell 'phoenician'. Unfortunately, the Persians were cleverer at making weapons. That's why you never meet Phoenicians any more.

Stone Age kids don't need to go to school anyway. They learn nearly everything by copying their parents. Which is a bit of a problem, really, because most Stone Age parents aren't very clever. If they see their kids about to do something stupid, like put their hand in the fire or eat a poison berry, they don't say – "Don't put your hand in the fire!" or "Don't eat that poison berry!" They just watch to see what happens. It's not because they are mean. It's because they haven't been to teachers' college.

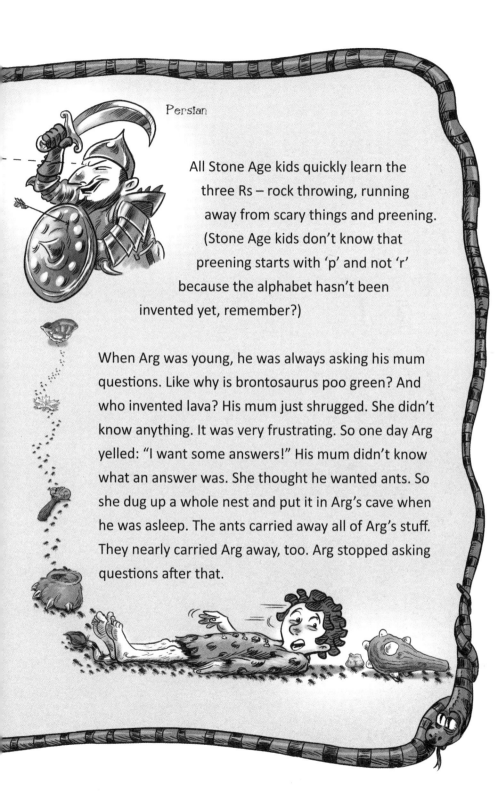

Persian

All Stone Age kids quickly learn the three Rs – rock throwing, running away from scary things and preening. (Stone Age kids don't know that preening starts with 'p' and not 'r' because the alphabet hasn't been invented yet, remember?)

When Arg was young, he was always asking his mum questions. Like why is brontosaurus poo green? And who invented lava? His mum just shrugged. She didn't know anything. It was very frustrating. So one day Arg yelled: "I want some answers!" His mum didn't know what an answer was. She thought he wanted ants. So she dug up a whole nest and put it in Arg's cave when he was asleep. The ants carried away all of Arg's stuff. They nearly carried Arg away, too. Arg stopped asking questions after that.

CHAPTER TWO

"It's terrible," said Skeet. "Just terrible."

"What's terrible?" asked Arg. He'd never seen Skeet looking so worried. His little arms were waving around madly.

"Everything," said Skeet. "Sometimes I wish I didn't have a big brain. Then I'd just be eating other dinosaurs instead of worrying about them."

"If you didn't have a big brain, we wouldn't be friends," said Arg.

Skeet breathed an enormous sigh. "I guess."

"Just tell me what's wrong," said Arg. "I'm sure there's nothing our two big brains can't fix."

Skeet shook his head. "I can't tell you. I'll have to show you. Climb on my back. It's a long way."

Advantages of having a T-rex for a friend

He's one friend you can easily beat at arm wrestling

You can fake your own death to get out of chores

He can clear crowds from your favourite beach

He's smart enough to get your jokes

Why do Grogllgrox have big nostrils?

Because they've got big fingers!

Skeet crashed through
the jungle. All Arg
could do was hold on
tight. When they reached
the Pterosaur Cliffs, Arg
got ready to climb off. It was the end of the
valley. He was very surprised when Skeet started
scrambling up a steep, rocky path.

By the time they reached the top, Skeet was
panting heavily.

"Do ... you ... see ...?" Skeet puffed.

The neighbouring valley was very different to Arg's valley. Instead of jungle, there was a vast plain of low-growing shrubs. Dotted among the shrubs were lots of large grey boulders.

"I don't see anything," said Arg. The valley seemed deserted.

"Keep ... looking ..." gasped Skeet.

Arg scanned left. Then right. What was he supposed to be looking for?

Suddenly a long, narrow shape rose into the air. Arg gaped in surprise. It looked like a giant snake. It swooped left, then right. Then flicked the air. Once. Twice.

CRACK! CRACK!

A sound like snapping branches echoed through the valley. It wasn't a snake. It was a tail. There was only one kind of tail that made a noise like that. Those weren't boulders. It was a herd of diplodocuses!

"What's wrong with them?" asked Arg.

"I don't know," said Skeet. "I came to get you as soon as I saw them."

"Maybe they're just sleeping," suggested Arg.

A large diplodocus struggled to its feet and stuck

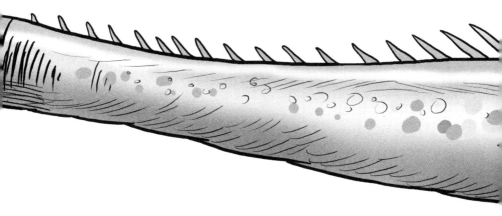

out its long neck and tail, trying to keep its balance.
It took three steps forward, shuffled left, then
toppled sideways. It was exactly how Arg walked
after Shlok rolled him down a hill in a hollow log.
That used to be their favourite game, until a log went
out of control and …

But that's another story.

"Something must be making them dizzy," said
Arg. "Let's go, Skeet!"

Dizzy Diplodocus

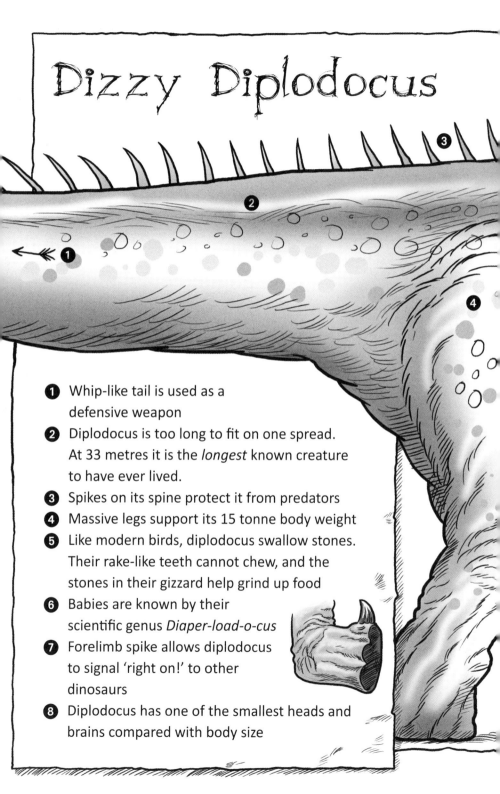

1. Whip-like tail is used as a defensive weapon
2. Diplodocus is too long to fit on one spread. At 33 metres it is the *longest* known creature to have ever lived.
3. Spikes on its spine protect it from predators
4. Massive legs support its 15 tonne body weight
5. Like modern birds, diplodocus swallow stones. Their rake-like teeth cannot chew, and the stones in their gizzard help grind up food
6. Babies are known by their scientific genus *Diaper-load-o-cus*
7. Forelimb spike allows diplodocus to signal 'right on!' to other dinosaurs
8. Diplodocus has one of the smallest heads and brains compared with body size

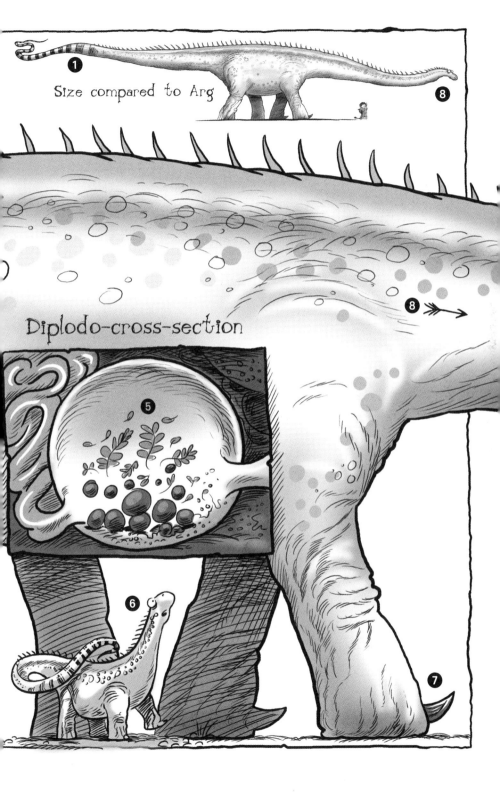

Size compared to Arg

Diplodo-cross-section

Arg held on tight. He expected Skeet to gallop
off down the hill. But Skeet didn't move. He stood
frozen on the spot, staring across the valley.
When Arg followed his gaze,
a shiver ran up his spine.

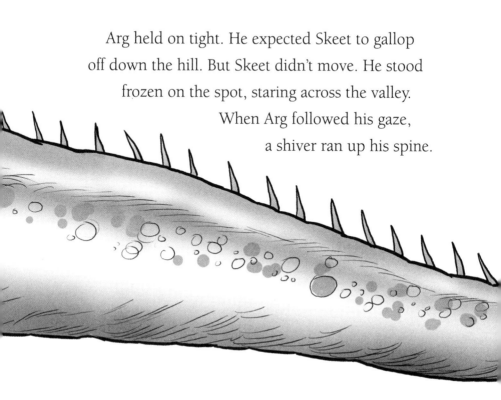

A Grogllgrox hunting party was winding its way
down a path on the far side. If they reached the dizzy
diplodocuses before Arg and Skeet, the whole herd
was doomed.

Most Stone Age hunters only killed as much meat

as they could carry. But not the Grogllgrox. They would kill every single diplodocus. Just for fun.

"I hope we're not too late already," said Skeet.

It was the first time Arg had ever heard Skeet sound scared.

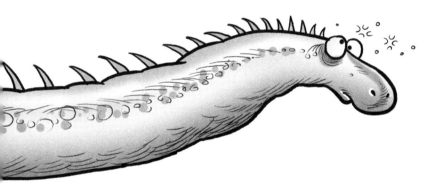

Arg had never been out of his valley before. His dad said it was too dangerous. But Arg wasn't afraid. Nothing could hurt him when he had a T-rex for a friend. They ploughed across the valley floor. This was no time to tiptoe.

The first diplodocus was
three spear throws away. It heard
them coming and lifted its long neck.
When it saw a cave boy riding a speeding
T-rex, it struggled to its feet. It twisted
round until it was facing away, but its only
defence was to swing its tail like a whip.

Its tail swung left. Then right. But as it
lifted skywards, the diplodocus lost its
balance and collapsed in a heap.

"Hurry up, Skeet!" yelled Arg.
They didn't have much time.

Instead of speeding up, Skeet started slowing down. He staggered left, then right, then came to a wobbly halt.

"What's wrong, Skeet?" asked Arg.

Skeet twisted his head. His eyes were rolling round and round in their sockets. And he had a strange, bewildered look on his face.

"Why is the world spinning?" asked Skeet.

Arg frowned. "The world's not spinning."

"Then it must be me," said Skeet.

Arg leapt clear as Skeet toppled sideways. A plume of dust rose into the air. It was like a big smoke signal in the sky.

Arg dusted himself off. His mouth was bone dry. It was easy being brave when you had a T-rex friend. But Skeet couldn't protect him now. Arg was all alone, far from home, in a strange valley full of dizzy dinosaurs. And the Grogllgrox hunting party would be there in no time.

Disadvantages of having a T-rex for a friend

What Dinosaurs really use their strange body parts for

Diplodocus use their long tails and necks to rest their weary legs — hammock style

Parasaurolophus hang their young in trees to keep them away from predators, or if they've been naughty

Shunosaurus like to play practical jokes
on dim-witted Neanderthals

Stygimoloch use
their chrome domes
to do head spins...

...especially when
they hang out with
veloci-rappers

CHAPTER THREE

"You've got to get up, Skeet!" yelled Arg. He grabbed Skeet's head and tried to lift it. But it was way too heavy. "If you don't hurry, the Grogllgrox will eat you ... and me!"

"I'll try," said Skeet. "But that smell ... can't you smell it?"

"I can't smell anything," sniffed Arg. "Now hurry up!"

Skeet closed his eyes and took a deep breath.

"You can do it, Skeet!" cheered Arg, as Skeet heaved his head off the ground. If Skeet charged the Grogllgrox, they were sure to run away. Not even Grogllgrox dared mess with a T-rex. Then they'd have time to figure out how to save the diplodocuses.

Skeet twisted and squirmed until he was back on his feet. "This way, Skeet!" said Arg.

Skeet didn't move. He stood there with his eyes firmly closed. His whole body kept swaying as if he might fall any second. He looked like Arg's dad after he'd been drinking too much fermented dinosaur milk.

Arg jiggled impatiently below. "We have to hurry, Skeet!"

"I'll be fine in a few seconds," said Skeet. He took a deep breath, then opened his eyes. "I just have to ..."

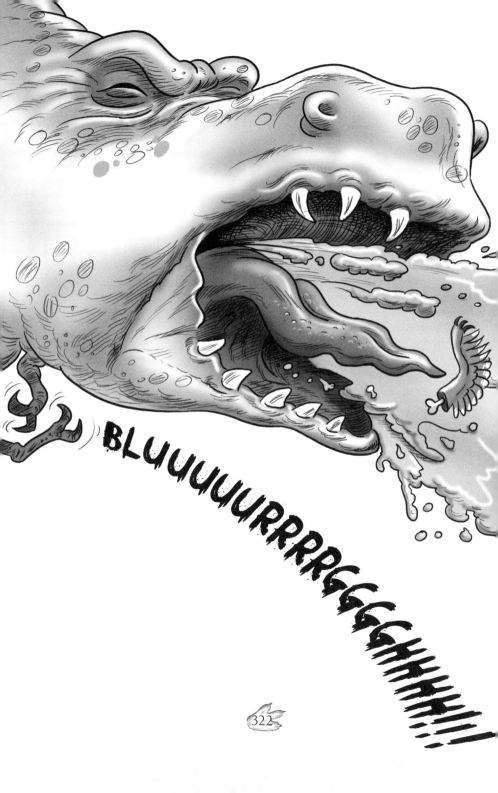

BLUUUUURRRRGGGGHHHH!!!!

322

A shower of chunky vomit splashed over Arg. Pieces of half-digested meat slid down Arg's back. Ragged bits of bone and scales stuck in his hair. He was glad he couldn't smell it.

"Urgh!" said Arg, wiping vomit from his face. "You could have warned me."

"Sorry," said Skeet, blushing. "I didn't mean to ..."

The second vomit was even bigger than the first. And runnier. It drenched Arg to the skin. It must have been very smelly, too, because the air was quickly turning black with swarms of madly buzzing flies.

"Oops!" said Skeet. Then he crashed to the ground.

Arg could hear Grogllgrox voices echoing across the valley. They sounded very excited. They must have noticed the dizzy diplodocuses. There was nothing Grogllgrox liked better than killing things.

Arg frantically paced backwards and forwards. There had to be some way of helping Skeet – or distracting the Grogllgrox. If only those stupid flies would go away! They were crawling in his hair, and over his face. There were flies up his nose and flies in his eyes. Every chunk of vomit was covered with flies fighting for their share.

It was impossible to think straight with all that ... loud ... buzzing?

Arg's footsteps slowed. That was strange. The buzzing was getting quieter. And quieter. Even stranger, the ground was now covered with flies. Arg scooped up a handful. They spun and buzzed in his hand, but didn't fly away. They weren't dead. They were dizzy, too!

Something was making everything dizzy. But why not him?

Arg stamped the ground in frustration. He heard a strange crackling sound. Then a cloud of grey dust shot into the air. As it swept up Arg's body, all the flies feasting on his vomit-soaked coat fell to the ground as though they'd been knocked out.

Arg knelt down. The ground was covered with strange pods. He pinched one between his fingers and it exploded in a shower of tiny spores. They made his eyes spin, but he didn't get dizzy.

It must be because I can't smell anything, thought Arg.

It was lucky his nose was full of snot, or he'd be lying there too.

An excited Grogllgrox cry drifted across the valley.

Arg smiled. He might just have a clever plan after all.

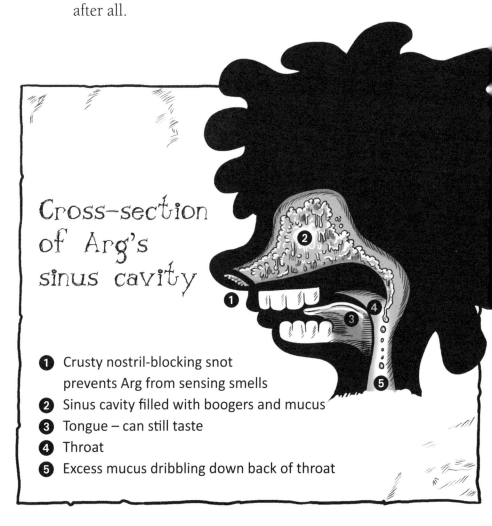

Cross-section of Arg's sinus cavity

1. Crusty nostril-blocking snot prevents Arg from sensing smells
2. Sinus cavity filled with boogers and mucus
3. Tongue – can still taste
4. Throat
5. Excess mucus dribbling down back of throat

Arg was so close he could hear the Grogllgrox
hunters' stomachs grumbling. The smell of fresh
game was making them hungry. Arg normally
wouldn't go anywhere near a Grogllgrox. They were
even more dangerous than Hng. If it wasn't for Skeet
and the dizzy diplodocuses, he'd be running away as
fast as he could. But his friend needed him.

There were eleven Grogllgroxes in the hunting party. They were making a huge racket, arguing and fighting with each other. If the diplodocuses weren't so dizzy, they'd be stampeding away before the hunters got close. The Grogllgrox were terrible at hunting. That's why they ate people.

Arg took a deep breath, then leapt to his feet. "Hey, you dumb cavemen!" he shouted. "You're ugly as an Ankylosaurus wart! That's why no one likes you!"

Popular Neanderthal Insults

May pus explode out of your ears like this

Maggot larvae are eating your brain

The Grogllgrox were so shocked, they stood grunting and scratching their bums. Nobody had ever insulted them before. Not to their faces, anyway. Most cave people ran away screaming as soon as they saw a Grogllgrox.

"Eww, pooh! I can smell your awful breath from here," yelled Arg. "What've you been doing? Have you been eating Grogllgrox brains again?"

The Grogllgrox swapped confused glances.

Finally, they all shrugged. Killing a cave boy might be a fun start to their day. They gave a blood-curdling scream, then sprinted towards Arg.

Arg set off across the plain, with the Grogllgrox close behind. With each heavy step, hundreds of tiny pods burst, spurting out spores. The air was soon thick with swirling grey clouds.

If the Grogllgrox had just walked, the dizzy dust

might not have reached their noses for ages. But the faster they ran, the quicker they'd get dizzy. At least that's what Arg hoped would happen.

Arg didn't look back. If his plan didn't work ...

There was a loud grunt of confusion. Then something heavy went crashing into a shrub. Arg smiled. It had to be one of the hunters. A second later there was another crash. Then a third. Arg kept running, keeping count all the way. When he got to ten, he risked a glance over his shoulder. One more dizzy Grogllgrox, and he was safe.

Arg's heart leapt into his throat. His plan had *almost* worked. The only problem was the eleventh chaser didn't have a nose! So he couldn't smell the dizzy dust either. And he was gaining ground with every step.

Grogllgrox kitchen nightmares

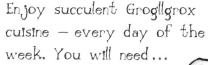

Enjoy succulent Grogllgrox
cuisine — every day of the
week. You will need...

One juicy
cave boy
brain

Some
potatoes

An onion or hot chilli

One rotten Dimorphodon egg

A branch of bay leaves
or other herbs

Recipe

1. Slice onions and chillies in half. Rub vigorously on your eyeballs. This will get you in the mood for some cooking.

2. Take your potatoes and throw them at anyone who tries to steal your fresh brain.

3. Strip bay leaves off stick.

4. Use stick to scratch bottom.

5. Scoop out brain.

6. Break rotten egg over brain.

7. Eat immediately before smell starts to fade.

8. Repeat step 4 as many times as you like.

Remember, you can dine in...

one scoop or two...?

...or take-away

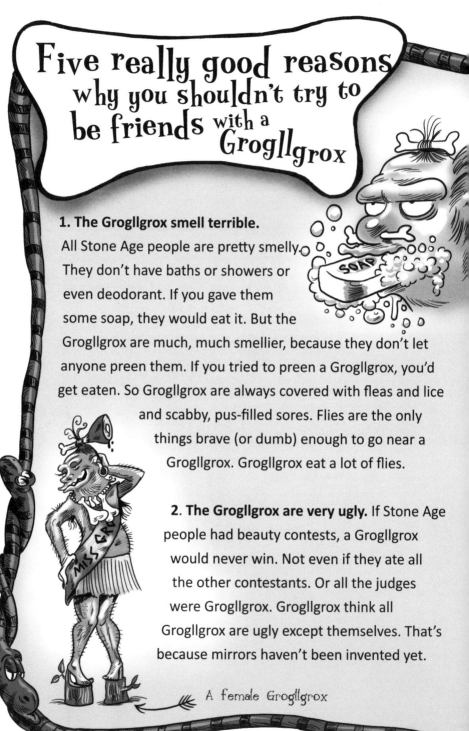

Five really good reasons why you shouldn't try to be friends with a Grogllgrox

1. The Grogllgrox smell terrible.

All Stone Age people are pretty smelly. They don't have baths or showers or even deodorant. If you gave them some soap, they would eat it. But the Grogllgrox are much, much smellier, because they don't let anyone preen them. If you tried to preen a Grogllgrox, you'd get eaten. So Grogllgrox are always covered with fleas and lice and scabby, pus-filled sores. Flies are the only things brave (or dumb) enough to go near a Grogllgrox. Grogllgrox eat a lot of flies.

2. The Grogllgrox are very ugly. If Stone Age people had beauty contests, a Grogllgrox would never win. Not even if they ate all the other contestants. Or all the judges were Grogllgrox. Grogllgrox think all Grogllgrox are ugly except themselves. That's because mirrors haven't been invented yet.

A female Grogllgrox

3. The Grogllgrox have no manners. If you invited Grogllgrox to your house, they wouldn't wipe their feet at the door. They'd leave a trail of muddy footprints across the carpet. They wouldn't even apologise. They wouldn't wash their hands before dinner. They wouldn't use cutlery, and would steal food off your plate.

If you tried to stop them, they would stab you with the fork. When they were finished, they would burp louder than your dad. If you turned your back for a second, they'd eat your cat and your goldfish.

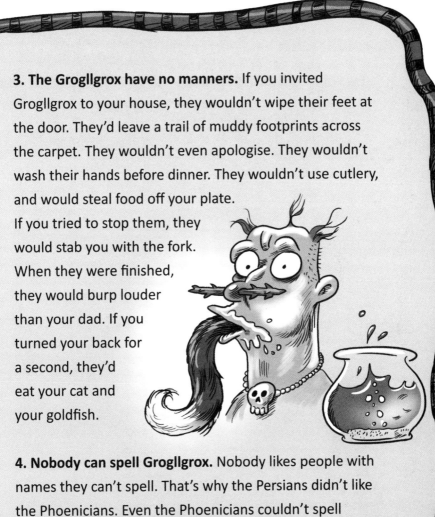

4. Nobody can spell Grogllgrox. Nobody likes people with names they can't spell. That's why the Persians didn't like the Phoenicians. Even the Phoenicians couldn't spell Grogllgrox, and they invented the alphabet.

5. The Grogllgrox would rather eat you than be your friend. So there's no point even *trying* to like them really, is there?

CHAPTER FOUR

Arg's lungs were heaving and his heart was racing faster than his feet. His brain was racing even faster. Any second now, the Grogllgrox's spear would come sailing through the air and pierce his heart. He hoped he died straight away. If the Grogllgrox caught him alive ...

No, that thought was even too terrifying to imagine.

He had to think of a new plan. Fast. Otherwise the Grogllgrox might take him back to their village and roast him on the fire. Or they might realise Arg had a big brain and force him to invent terrible new weapons so they could defeat all the other tribes and take over the world. Or they might eat only a bit of

his brain and turn him into a zombie ... except
zombies hadn't been invented yet.

Manners when dining with a Grogllgrox

Make sure to chew your food with your mouth open and talk while you are eating

Concentrate! thought Arg. That was the problem with having a big brain. He could think of a million different things that might happen. If only he could think of some way of escaping from a nose-less Grogllgrox.

Maybe the Grogllgrox would show mercy? Arg was only a boy, after all.

What a stupid idea! Arg scolded himself. *Grogllgrox never show mercy!*

Arg's steps began to slow. His legs felt as if they were turning to stone. When he couldn't run another step, he spun around to face his chaser.

If he was going to get caught, he'd at least put up a fight.

Arg was very surprised to discover that there was no grinning, nose-less Grogllgrox closing in for the kill. The Grogllgrox was trailing way behind. It wasn't because Arg was so fast or because the Grogllgrox was getting dizzy. It was because he'd spotted a much more valuable prey.

A huge T-rex, lying helpless on the ground.

Killing a T-rex was the bravest thing a Grogllgrox could do. If he went back to his village with a T-rex jawbone, they would probably make him the leader of the tribe. Nobody would ever know that Skeet had been too dizzy to defend himself.

Arg could hear Skeet moaning loudly. Skeet wasn't even aware that there was a Grogllgrox heading straight towards him. Arg had to warn him! He rushed through the shrubs, keeping as low as possible. If the Grogllgrox saw him too early, he might spear Arg first and kill Skeet second.

The Grogllgrox wasn't taking any chances. He cautiously circled around, creeping closer and closer.

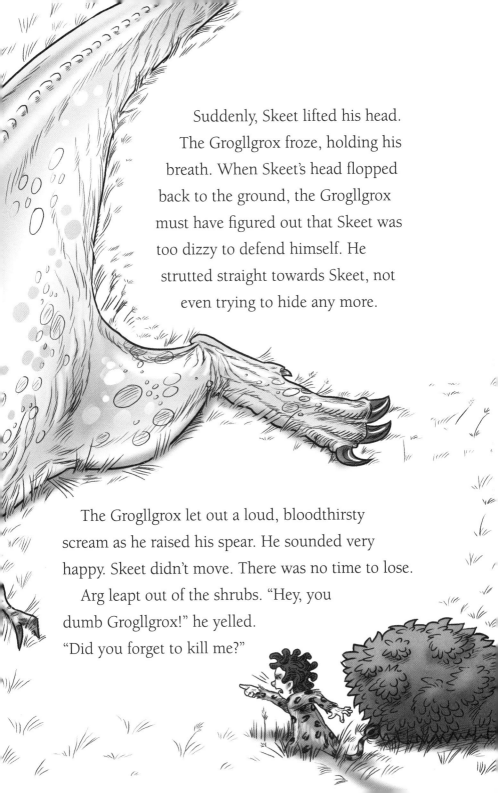

Suddenly, Skeet lifted his head. The Grogllgrox froze, holding his breath. When Skeet's head flopped back to the ground, the Grogllgrox must have figured out that Skeet was too dizzy to defend himself. He strutted straight towards Skeet, not even trying to hide any more.

The Grogllgrox let out a loud, bloodthirsty scream as he raised his spear. He sounded very happy. Skeet didn't move. There was no time to lose.

Arg leapt out of the shrubs. "Hey, you dumb Grogllgrox!" he yelled. "Did you forget to kill me?"

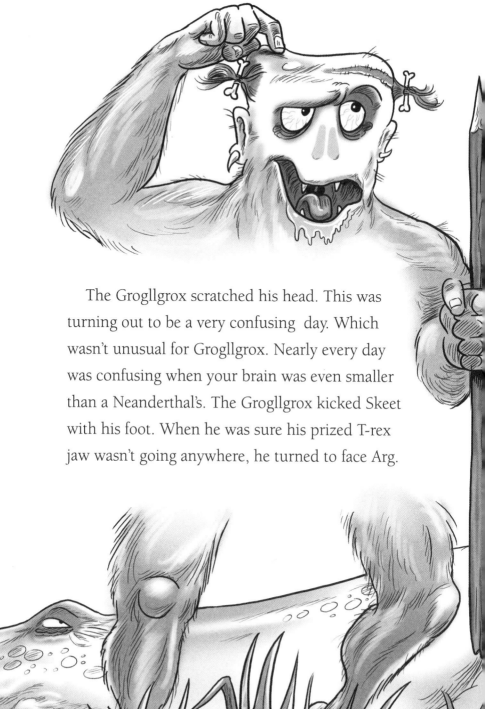

The Grogllgrox scratched his head. This was turning out to be a very confusing day. Which wasn't unusual for Grogllgrox. Nearly every day was confusing when your brain was even smaller than a Neanderthal's. The Grogllgrox kicked Skeet with his foot. When he was sure his prized T-rex jaw wasn't going anywhere, he turned to face Arg.

"You're so dumb you even forgot to put on your nose!" yelled Arg.

The Grogllgrox frowned and rubbed his missing nose. Then he gave another bloodthirsty scream. He stalked towards Arg, waving his spear.

Arg had never been so close to a Grogllgrox before. It was very scary. He felt like running away. Fast. But he couldn't leave Skeet.

Arg tried to speak, but his mouth felt like it was full of sand. Only a squeak escaped.

The Grogllgrox smiled. It made Hng's smiles look friendly. The Grogllgrox's teeth were rotting and broken. The front teeth had been filed down to points.

"You don't scare me," squeaked Arg.

Over the Grogllgrox's shoulder, Arg saw Skeet squirming in the dirt. As Skeet hauled himself to his feet, Arg gritted his teeth. He wasn't beaten yet.

Arg crouched low, ready to fight the Grogllgrox. If he could delay him just a few valuable seconds, Skeet might recover. It was their only chance.

The Grogllgrox smiled and raised his spear. He didn't believe in fighting fair. He didn't notice Skeet staggering towards him until a huge T-rex-shaped shadow spilled across the ground. The Grogllgrox's eyes flew open and his jaw dropped as he turned. But he was too late.

CHOMP!

Skeet tossed his head back and swallowed one half of the Grogllgrox whole. The other half teetered for a second, then fell forward into the dirt.

Arg was very relieved to see his friend standing again. Even more relieved to still be alive. He raced over and hugged Skeet's leg.

"Thanks, Skeet!" he cheered. "That was close."

"You're welcome," mumbled Skeet. His legs were wobbly, and his face was the colour of ashes.

"That's what friends ..."

BLUUUURRRGGGHHHH!!

A spray of stinky liquid drenched Arg. Again. It looked like his Mum's algae soup and probably smelt almost as bad. Arg was glad he couldn't smell it. Skeet retched again. Bits of half-chewed Grogllgrox tumbled to the ground in a mangled mess. Then Skeet sprawled forward, face first, in a pool of vomit.

Arg started to breath a sigh of relief. But it choked halfway down his throat as a ferocious war-cry drifted down from the hills. Another Grogllgrox hunting party was winding its way into the valley. They weren't safe yet!

CHAPTER FIVE

Arg sagged down onto Skeet's shoulder. He was too exhausted to move. There was no way he could repeat his plan to distract the Grogllgrox. And his brain was too tired to think of a new plan.

The sound of crashing footsteps barged into Arg's thoughts. One of the dizzy Grogllgroxes had managed to drag himself to his feet. He was lumbering straight towards Arg. His bloodshot eyes were spinning in their sockets as he raised his spear. Arg didn't have the strength to move. He clenched his teeth and screwed up his eyes. This was going to hurt.

WHOOOOOOOSSSSSSHHHHH!

Skeet's tail swept along the ground in a whirlwind of dust and insects. It slammed into the Grogllgrox, sending him flying.

"Pesky Grogllgrox," chuckled Skeet.

"You're getting better!" cheered Arg. Skeet's eyes weren't spinning any more. He'd stopped vomiting, too. That was a good sign.

But Skeet shook his head. "Not quickly enough, I'm afraid," he said. "Those Grogllgrox are going to be here soon. You better leave now, Arg, while you still can." Then he closed his eyes with a sigh.

Arg knew Skeet was right. The Grogllgrox hunting party was already halfway down the path. If he didn't leave now, they'd kill him, along with Skeet and all the diplodocuses. But no matter how many times his brain told him to leave, his feet refused to obey. There had to be *something* he could do.

A big bug buzzed down and landed on Arg's chin. His reflex was to swipe it away. But his brain stopped his hand just in time. It wasn't just any bug. It was a stink bug. Just like the ones Hng used for her prank. A second later, another bug latched onto his hair. Then a third bug landed on his hand.

The whole area was swirling with stink bugs. They must have been hiding in the bushes and

Skeet's swooshing tail had disturbed them. Now they
were all coming back to land. And most of them
were landing on Arg.

When he was completely covered in stink bugs,
Arg took a deep breath, puffing himself upright.
Maybe there was a way to get the diplodocuses and
Skeet on their feet again after all. It was a long shot.
If it worked, he'd have his sister, Hng, to thank.
If it *didn't* work, it would be too late to escape.

The diplodocus herd was strung out in a long line, all facing in the same direction. A large male was at each end. In between were females and young. They must have been migrating across the valley before they got dizzy.

Arg walked gingerly to the front of the line. He wasn't worried about disturbing the diplodocuses.

He didn't want to frighten the stink bugs. If they flew off, his plan was ruined.

The lead diplodocus moaned when Arg appeared beside it. But it didn't move. Arg carefully plucked two stink bugs off his coat. He held them in front of the diplodocus's snout. Then ...

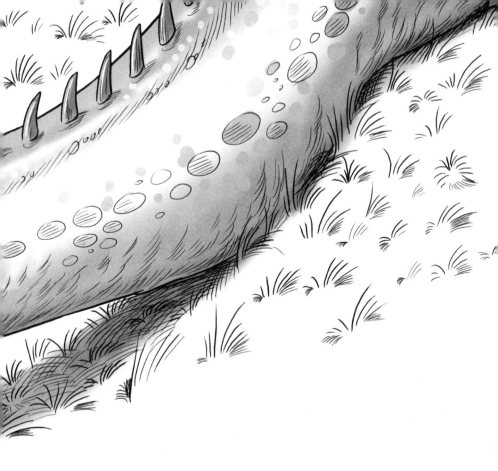

The stink bugs exploded, spurting yellow goo up
the diplodocus's nostrils. Arg scuttled backwards. If
the diplodocus went crazy, he could be crushed.
Luckily the diplodocus didn't panic. It flipped onto
its feet and stretched its long neck. Then it flicked
its long tail.

CRACK! CRACK!

Grogllgrox war cries rumbled down the hillside.
They weren't going to let easy prey get away.
There was no time to lose. Arg ran along the line
of diplodocuses, bursting stink bugs in their noses.
Each time, the diplodocus flipped onto its feet.
They didn't stampede. They just stood there,
whipping their tails.

CRACK! CRACK!

The faster Arg ran, the more stink bugs fluttered away. By the time he reached the last diplodocus, there were only two stink bugs left. He popped them under the diplodocus's nose. It leapt to its feet.

CRACK! CRACK!

The Grogllgrox reached the valley floor. They charged towards the diplodocuses, waving their spears and making a racket.

The frightened diplodocuses took off, leaving the Grogllgrox puffing in their dust.

Arg shook his head. The Grogllgrox really were terrible hunters.

Finally, the Grogllgrox noticed Arg. They raced towards him, grinning fiendishly. A cave boy was much easier prey. Tastier, too.

Arg hurried over to Skeet. He frisked his coat, looking for stink bugs. But they'd all flown off.

"Get up, Skeet!" yelled Arg.

Skeet snored a reply. He was fast asleep.

Suddenly a big stink bug landed on Skeet's back. Arg leapt on it and shoved it up Skeet's nostril.

He hooked an arm around Skeet's neck,
then punched Skeet's nose. Hard.

Skeet bolted to his feet and started spinning in wild circles. Arg held on like he was riding a bucking bronco in a rodeo ... except rodeos hadn't been invented yet.

"Pooh! Pooh!" Skeet yelled. His tiny arms flopped uselessly, trying to reach his snout, while his swinging tail sent one Grogllgrox after another tumbling into the bushes.

The remaining Grogllgrox screamed and ran away.

"Let's get out of here, Skeet!" yelled Arg. Skeet set off as fast as his legs could carry him, trying to escape the terrible smell. He didn't slow down until they were back at Arg's village.

"We make a good team," said Arg, as he climbed down.

"That's because we're good friends," said Skeet. "Now, if you'll excuse me, I'm going to stick my nose in the Slime Ooze Pit."

Arg was very happy to be home. He was even happy to see Hng. If she hadn't had the idea to use stink bugs, he'd be in a Grogllgrox stew by now.

Hng was very surprised when Arg gave her a huge hug; crackle crackle crackle

The pods that were stuck to Arg's coat popped, puffing spores in Hng's face. Her eyes started spinning, then she toppled sideways.

Arg sighed. Being nice to your sister was never a good idea.

NEED MORE NEANDERTHAL NONSENSE? VISIT OUR WEBSITE WWW.DINOSAUR-RESCUE.COM

Check it out on your
laprock or tablet for
crazy Dinosaur Rescue
facts, trailers, downloads,
free sample chapters,
and more ...

PRAISE FOR DINOSAUR RESCUE

*"This book is perfect for all those who
don't believe that reading can be fun."*
Trevor Agnew, The Source

"… boy readers in particular are going to love this series."
Book Council of NZ School Library

*"Really gross, full of revolting, slapstick humour
and facts, and featuring hilarious illustrations
and diagrams on almost every page, this new series
is a winner for boys, especially, aged 6 plus …"*
Magpies Magazine

MEET THE

Kyle Mewburn
(A-Kyle-o-saurus)

What's your favourite dinosaur? The one that's the furtherest away from me.

What's the most stupid thing you did as a kid? Went to skool ... um, I mean school.

What's the most disgusting thing you've ever eaten? A freshly caught sea urchin a Greek fisherman offered me. I was too polite to say no.

What's the most dangerous thing you ever did? Went camping in a cyclone. Luckily my tent really *was* cyclone-proof.

What's the most embarrassing thing that ever happened to you? I've never been abducted by an alien. Which is actually something that *never* happened to me, but still, it's pretty embarrassing to think no alien thinks I'm worth abducting.

CREATORS

Donovan Bixley
(Don-o-saurus)

What's your favourite dinosaur? Styracosaurus.

What's the most stupid thing you did as a kid? I did
a back flip off the monkey bars and everyone cheered.
So I did it again and broke both my arms. Back in those
Neanderthal days, the playground was concrete!

What's the most disgusting thing you've ever eaten?
I lived in Indonesia as a kid and once ate a deep-fried
chicken leg, which turned out to be a chicken head!

What's the most dangerous thing you ever did?
Probably windsurfing in 6-metre high waves. I thought
I was going to die that day.

**What's the most embarrassing thing that's ever
happened to you?** My mum once made me home-made
underwear. They fell apart in the changing room after PE
one day.

KEEP YOUR EYE OUT FOR THE ALL-NEW

DINOSAUR RESCUE BOOK OF STUFF

STUFFED with lots of activities

silly stuff

DINOSTROLOGY
Star signs of the dinosaurs

T-rex
January 21 – February 19
Your aggressive looks keep others away and you find it hard to grasp situations (because of your puny arms). But inside you're really a big softie (especially your liver and intestines).

Dakosaurus
March 21 – April 20
Your big mouth often gets you into trouble with your friends and family – you just can't help eating everyone!

Di...
Feb...
Yo...

Spino...
May 22 ...
You're o... up. Don... biggest carnivore who e...

Microraptor
June 22 – July 23
You're a forward thinking individual who imagines a world where things have evolved, ...ur friends

Plesiosaur
July 24 – August 23
Your friends think you're high strung – always prone to flip out when you get swamped. Just chill out dude – ...u live at the beach!

Arg's dream tree-house

1 Flying fox made from gigantoraptor wishbone

2 Bearskin hammock for summer nights

3 Mosquito net, woven by specially trained spiders

4 Diving board made from argentinosaurus rib

5 Nearby cave for Skeet to sleep in

6 Cactus Maze to keep out Hng and intruders. See page ?? to see if you can solve it

7 Pool

8 Stairs to hammock and flying fox

continued on next page …

cool stuff

HAVE YOU GOT ALL THE DINOSAUR RESCUE BOOKS?